UTOPIA
Student Literature

Center for Gifted Education
School of Education
The College of William and Mary

W&M Center for Gifted Education

Unit Developer: Mary Ann Yedinak

KENDALL/HUNT PUBLISHING COMPANY
4050 Westmark Drive Dubuque, Iowa 52002

Cover photo courtesy of Corel.

Book Team

Chairman and Chief Executive Officer: Mark C. Falb
Vice President, Director of National Book Program: Alfred C. Grisanti
Editorial Development Supervisor: Georgia Botsford
Developmental Editor: Angela Willenbring
Prepress Project Coordinator: Sheri Hosek
Prepress Editor: Carrie Maro
Permissions Editor: Colleen Zelinsky
Design Manager: Jodi Splinter

Author Information for Correspondence and Workshops:

Center for Gifted Education
The College of William and Mary
P.O. Box 8795
Williamsburg, VA 23187-8795
Phone: 757-221-2362
Email address: cfge@wm.edu
Web address: www.cfge.wm.edu

ISBN 0-7872-9393-8

Printed in the United States of America
10 9 8 7 6 5 4 3 2 1

CONTENTS

Short Stories/Essays

The Ones Who Walk Away from Omelas
Ursula K. LeGuin 1

Utopia: The Search for a Perfect Society
Jeffrey Stroebel 5

Harrison Bergeron
Kurt Vonnegut 13

Trurl's Machine
Stanislaw Lem 17

The Veldt
Ray Bradbury 23

The Unicorn Man of India
James Cross Giblin 31

Barbie-Q
Sandra Cisneros 33

Fool's Paradise
Isaac Bashevis Singer 35

The Censors
Luisa Valenzuela 39

The Man That Corrupted Hadleyburg
Mark Twain 41

Poetry

Happiness
Priscilla Leonard 65

Before I Could Call Myself Ángel Gonzáles
Ángel Gonzáles 67

The Future
Ángel Gonzáles 69

Now That Time Seems All Mine
Patrizia Cavalli 71

Far From Kingdoms
Patrizia Cavalli 73

Middle Class Blues
Hans Magnus Enzensberger 75

Songs for Those Who Know
Hans Magnus Enzensberger 77

Assembly Line
Shu Ting 79

Gifts
Shu Ting 81

Fairy Tales
Shu Ting 83

Hold Fast Your Dreams
Louise Driscoll 85

Harlem
Langston Hughes 87

My Heart Leaps Up
William Wordsworth 89

Daffodils
William Wordsworth 91

Spring
Thomas Nashe 93

People Liked Him
Edgar Guest 95

If
Rudyard Kipling 97

A Perfect Day
Carrie Jacobs Bond 99

Do Not Go Gentle into That Good Night
Dylan Thomas 101

The Ones Who Walk Away from Omelas

Ursula K. LeGuin

With a clamor of bells that set the swallows soaring, the Festival of Summer came to the city Omelas, bright-towered by the sea. The rigging of the boats in harbor sparkled with flags. In the streets between houses with red roofs and painted walls, between old moss-grown gardens and under avenues of trees, past great parks and public buildings, processions moved. Some were decorous: old people in long stiff robes of mauve and grey, grave master workmen, quiet, merry women carrying their babies and chatting as they walked. In other streets the music beat faster, a shimmering of gong and tambourine, and the people went dancing, the procession was a dance. Children dodged in and out, their high calls rising like the swallows' crossing flights over the music and the singing. All the processions wound towards the north side of the city, where on the great water-meadow called the Green Fields boys and girls, naked in the bright air, with mud-stained feet and ankles and long, lithe arms, exercised their restive horses before the race. The horses wore no gear at all but a halter without bit. Their manes were braided with streamers of silver, gold, and green. They flared their nostrils and pranced and boasted to one another; they were vastly excited, the horse being the only animal who has adopted our ceremonies as his own. Far off to the north and west the mountains stood up half encircling Omelas on her bay. The air of morning was so clear that the snow still crowning the Eighteen Peaks burned with white-gold fire across the miles of sunlit air, under the dark blue of the sky. There was just enough wind to make the banners that marked the racecourse snap and flutter now and then. In the silence of the broad green meadows one could hear the music winding through the city streets, farther and nearer and ever approaching, a cheerful faint sweetness of the air that from time to time trembled and gathered together and broke out into the great joyous clanging of the bells.

Joyous! How is one to tell about joy? How describe the citizens of Omelas?

They were not simple folk, you see, though they were happy. But we do not say the words of cheer much any more. All smiles have become archaic. Given a description such as this one tends to make certain assumptions. Given a description such as this one tends to look next for the King, mounted on a splendid stallion and surrounded by his noble knights, or perhaps in a golden litter borne by great-muscled slaves. But there was no king. They did not use swords, or keep slaves. They were not barbarians. I do not know the rules and laws of their society, but I suspect that they were singularly few. As they did without monarchy and slavery, so they also got on without the stock exchange, the advertisement, the secret police, and the bomb. Yet I repeat that these were not simple folk, not dulcet shepherds, noble savages, bland utopians. They were not less complex than us. The trouble is that we have a bad habit, encouraged by pedants and sophisticates, of considering happiness as something rather stupid. Only pain is intellectual, only evil interesting. This is the treason of the artist: a refusal to admit the banality of evil and the terrible boredom of pain. If you can't lick 'em, join 'em. If it hurts, repeat it. But to praise despair is to condemn delight, to embrace violence is to lose hold of everything else. We have almost lost hold; we can no longer describe a happy man, nor make any celebration of joy. How can I tell you about the people of Omelas? They were not naïve and happy children—though their children were, in fact, happy.

They were mature, intelligent, passionate adults whose lives were not wretched. O miracle! but I wish I could describe it better. I wish I could convince you. Omelas sounds in my words like a city in a fairy tale, long ago and far away, once upon a time. Perhaps it would be best if you imagined it as your own fancy bids, assuming it will rise to the occasion, for certainly I cannot suit you all. For instance, how about technology? I think that there would be no cars or helicopters in and above the streets; this follows from the fact that the people of Omelas are happy people. Happiness is based on a just discrimination of what is necessary, what is neither necessary nor destructive, and what is destructive. In the middle category, however—that of the unnecessary but undestructive, that of comfort, luxury, exuberance, etc.—they could perfectly well have central heating, subway trains, washing machines, and all kinds of marvelous devices not yet invented here, floating light-sources, fuelless power, a cure for the common cold. Or they could have none of that: it doesn't matter. As you like it. I inclined to think that people from towns up and down the coast have been coming in to Omelas during the last days before the Festival on very fast little trains and double-decked trams, and that the train station of Omelas is actually the handsomest building in town, though plainer than the magnificent Farmers' Market. But even granted trains, I fear that Omelas so far strikes some of you as goody-goody. Smiles, bells, parades, horses, bleh. If so, please add an orgy. If an orgy would help, don't hesitate. Let us not, however, have temples from which issue beautiful nude priests and priestesses already half in ecstasy and ready to copulate with any man or woman, lover or stranger, who desires union with the deep godhead of the blood, although that was my first idea. But really it would be better not to have any temples in Omelas—at least, not manned temples. Religion yes, clergy no. Surely the beautiful nudes can just wander about, offering themselves like divine soufflés to the hunger of the needy and the rapture of the flesh. Let them join the processions. Let tambourines be struck above the copulations, and the glory of desire be proclaimed upon the gongs, and (a not unimportant point) let the offspring of these delightful rituals be beloved and looked after by all. One thing I know there is none of in Omelas is guilt. But what else should there be? I thought at first there were no drugs, but that is puritanical. For those who like it, the faint insistent sweetness of *drooz* may perfume the ways of the city, *drooz* which first brings a great lightness and brilliance to the mind and limbs, and then after some hours a dreamy languor, and wonderful visions at last of the very arcana and inmost secrets of the Universe, as well as exciting the pleasure of sex beyond all belief; and it is not habit-forming. For more modest tastes I think there ought to be beer. What else, what else belongs in the joyous city? The sense of victory, surely, the celebration of courage. But as we did without clergy, let us do without soldiers. The joy built upon successful slaughter is not the right kind of joy; it will not do; it is fearful and it is trivial. A boundless and generous contentment, a magnanimous triumph felt not against some outer enemy but in communion with the finest and fairest in the souls of all men everywhere and the splendor of the world's summer: this is what swells the hearts of the people of Omelas, and the victory they celebrate is that of life. I really don't think many of them need to take *drooz.*

Most of the processions have reached the Green Fields by now. A marvelous smell of cooking goes forth from the red and blue tents of the provisioners. The faces of small children are amiably sticky; in the benign grey beard of a man a couple of crumbs of rich pastry are entangled. The youths and girls have mounted their horses and are beginning to group around the starting line of the course. An old woman, small, fat, and laughing, is passing out flowers from a basket, and tall young men wear her flowers in their shining hair. A child of nine or ten sits at the edge of the crowd, alone, playing on a wooden flute. People pause to listen, and they smile, but they do not speak to him, for he never ceases playing and never sees them, his dark eyes wholly rapt in the sweet, thin magic of the tune.

He finishes, and slowly lowers his hands holding the wooden flute.

As if that little private silence were the signal, all at once a trumpet sounds from the pavilion near the starting line: imperious, melancholy, piercing. The horses rear on their slender legs, and some of them neigh in answer. Sober-faced, the young riders stroke the horses' necks and soothe them, whispering, "Quiet, quiet, there my beauty, my hope. . . ." They begin to form in rank along the starting line. The crowds along the racecourse are like a field of grass and flowers in the wind. The Festival of Summer has begun.

Do you believe? Do you accept the festival, the city, the joy? No? Then let me describe one more thing.

In a basement under one of the beautiful public buildings of Omelas, or perhaps in the cellar of one of its spacious private homes, there is a room. It has one locked door, and no window. A little light seeps in dustily between cracks in the boards, secondhand from a cobwebbed window somewhere across the cellar. In one corner of the little room a couple of mops, with stiff, clotted, foul-smelling heads, stand near a rusty bucket. The floor is dirt, a little damp to the touch, as cellar dirt usually is. The room is about three paces long and two wide: a mere broom closet or disused tool room. In the room a child is sitting. It could be a boy or a girl. It looks about six, but actually is nearly ten. It is feeble-minded. Perhaps it was born defective, or perhaps it has become imbecile through fear, malnutrition, and neglect. It picks its nose and occasionally fumbles vaguely with its toes or genitals, as it sits hunched in the corner farthest from the bucket and the two mops. It is afraid of the mops. It finds them horrible. It shuts its eyes, but it knows the mops are still standing there; and the door is locked; and nobody will come. The door is always locked; and nobody ever comes, except that sometimes—the child has no understanding of time or interval—sometimes the door rattles terribly and opens, and a person, or several people, are there. One of them may come in and kick the child to make it stand up. The others never come close, but peer in at it with frightened, disgusted eyes. The food bowl and the water jug are hastily filled, the door is locked, the eyes disappear. The people at the door never say anything, but the child, who has not always lived in the tool room, and can remember sunlight and its mother's voice, sometimes speaks. "I will be good," it says. "Please let me out. I will be good!" They never answer. The child used to scream for help at night, and cry a good deal, but now it only makes a kind of whining, "eh-haa, eh-haa," and it speaks less and less often. It is so thin there are no calves to its legs; its belly protrudes; it lives on a half-bowl of corn meal and grease a day. It is naked. Its buttocks and thighs are a mass of festered sores, as it sits in its own excrement continually.

They all know it is there, all the people of Omelas. Some of them have come to see it, others are content merely to know it is there. They all know that it has to be there. Some of them understand why, and some do not, but they all understand that their happiness, the beauty of their city, the tenderness of their friendships, the health of their children, the wisdom of their scholars, the skill of their makers, even the abundance of their harvest and the kindly weathers of their skies, depend wholly on this child's abominable misery.

This is usually explained to children when they are between eight and twelve, whenever they seem capable of understanding; and most of those who come to see the child are young people, though often enough an adult comes, or comes back, to see the child. No matter how well the matter has been explained to them, these young spectators are always shocked and sickened at the sight. They feel disgust, which they had thought themselves superior to. They feel anger, outrage, impotence, despite all the explanations. They would like to do something for the child. But there is nothing they can do. If the child were brought up into the sunlight out of that vile place, if it were cleaned and fed and comforted, that would be a good thing, indeed; but if it were done, in that day and hour all the prosperity and beauty and delight of Omelas would wither and be destroyed. Those are the terms. To exchange all the goodness and grace of every life in Omelas for that single, small improvement: to throw away the happiness of thousands for the chance of the happiness of one: that would be to let guilt within the walls indeed.

The terms are strict and absolute; there may not even be a kind word spoken to the child.

Often the young people go home in tears, or in a tearless rage, when they have seen the child and faced this terrible paradox. They may brood over it for weeks or years. But as time goes on they begin to realize that even if the child could be released, it would not get much good of its freedom: a little vague pleasure of warmth and food, no doubt, but little more. It is too degraded and imbecile to know any real joy. It has been afraid too long ever to be free of fear. Its habits are too uncouth for it to respond to humane treatment. Indeed, after so long it would probably be wretched without walls about it to protect it, and darkness for its eyes, and its own excrement to sit in. Their tears at the bitter injustice dry when they begin to perceive the terrible justice of reality, and to accept it. Yet it is their tears and anger, the trying of their generosity and the acceptance of their helplessness, which are perhaps the true source of the splendor of their lives. Theirs is no vapid, irresponsible happiness. They know that they, like the child, are not free. They know compassion. It is the existence of the child, and their knowledge of its existence, that makes possible the nobility of their architecture, the poignancy of their music, the profundity of their science. It is because of the child that they are so gentle with children. They know that if the wretched one were not there snivelling in the dark, the other one, the flute-player, could make no joyful music as the young riders line up in their beauty for the race in the sunlight of the first morning of summer.

Now do you believe in them? Are they not more credible? But there is one more thing to tell, and this is quite incredible.

At times one of the adolescent girls or boys who go to see the child does not go home to weep or rage, does not, in fact, go home at all. Sometimes also a man or woman much older falls silent for a day or two, and then leaves home. These people go out into the street, and walk down the street alone. They keep walking, and walk straight out of the city of Omelas, through the beautiful gates. They keep walking across the farmlands of Omelas. Each one goes alone, youth or girl, man or woman. Night falls; the traveler must pass down village streets, between the houses with yellow-lit windows, and on out into the darkness of the fields. Each alone, they go west or north, towards the mountains. They go on. They leave Omelas, they walk ahead into the darkness, and they do not come back. The place they go towards is a place even less imaginable to most of us than the city of happiness. I cannot describe it at all. It is possible that it does not exist. But they seem to know where they are going, the ones who walk away from Omelas.

Utopia: The Search for a Perfect Society

Jeffrey Stroebel

The term *utopia* was first used as a title of a book by Thomas More, published in 1516.[1] Utopia is derived from the Greek *ou topus* meaning nowhere. More is one of the most respected men in British history. A close friend of the famous Dutch scholar Erasmus, he was one of the leading figures in the British Renaissance even prior to the publication of *Utopia*. More was trained as a lawyer, elected a Member of Parliament, and eventually became a top advisor to King Henry VIII. Deeply religious, More refused to accept Henry's divorce of his first wife, Catherine of Aragon, and abandonment of the Catholic Church. As a result, he was imprisoned in the Tower of London and eventually beheaded in 1535 on a charge of treason. More's principled opposition to the king has been immortalized in the play *A Man for All Seasons,* and he was made a saint of the Catholic Church upon the four hundredth anniversary of his death in 1935.

More's novel *Utopia* is a conversational narrative. It begins when More was sent by Henry VIII to Flanders to negotiate matters related to the cloth trade. While there he was introduced by a friend to Raphael Hythloday, an old Portuguese mariner who had sailed on many fascinating journeys, often while accompanying the legendary explorer Amerigo Vespucci.[2] Hythloday proceeded to tell more of one of his journeys to a far off land called Utopia. Utopia was an island located directly opposite England on the globe. The crescent shaped island had a narrow strait separating the two ends of the crescent. Dangerous reefs and shallows made it almost impossible for sailors unfamiliar with the area to penetrate the strait. In addition, the strait was defended by a fortress built into a huge rock at the entrance to the strait.

The key societal feature of Utopia was that there was no personal property. Hythloday related that the Utopians believed that all evil stemmed from the ambition of man to accumulate personal wealth and property; "no equal and just distribution of things can be made, nor that perfect wealth shall ever be among men, unless this property be exiled and banished." At this point, More argued with Hythloday, pointing out that the abolition of private ownership would also result in the end of personal ambition, and that laziness would be the only logical result if man were allowed to rely on others' labor for his well being. Hythloday's response was only to describe the happiness of the Utopians: "no man has anything, yet every man is rich." The Utopians also ignored European symbols of wealth. Everyone wore similar, plain clothing. Precious metals such as gold and silver were used only to make chamber pots and chains for slaves and criminals. Some children wore jewels, but any adult who wore them was ridiculed for being childish.

The island of Utopia was divided into fifty-four identical city-states of approximately 6,000 citizens each. High defensive walls surrounded the cities, which were made up of three-story, connected buildings. Citizens lived in houses facing a street with large gardens in the back. A mayor, chosen by elected people's representatives, governed the city-states. The mayor served for life, unless he was convicted of being a tyrant. Each of the city-states also elected three men to represent them for a one-year period on the island's governing assembly. This assembly met only once per year. All elections were by secret ballot, and any candidate who openly campaigned or solicited votes was immediately disqualified. Laws were

[1]*Utopia* was published in Latin.
[2]The Name Hythloday is taken from the Greek *Hythlodaeus,* meaning "dispenser of non-sense."

passed only after a minimum of three days of open discussion. Any public official who was found guilty of trying to influence decisions in private was charged with the crime of political conspiracy and received the death penalty. Hythloday told More that Utopia's system of government had proven so popular that other countries had asked Utopians to come and rule them.

The family was the key unit in Utopian society. Families were large and extended, consisting of ten to sixteen adults. Men were allowed to marry at age twenty-two, women at eighteen. Premarital sex was strongly punished, with the participants forbidden ever to marry. Prior to marriage, however, the young man and woman were brought in front of each other naked so that they could examine the body of the one they intended to marry. Marriages were considered lifetime commitments and adultery was punished by slavery. Wives were expected to be subservient to their husbands. Children were removed from the family early in their lives for their education, which was conducted by elected public officials. Every student was exposed to classic literature and also taught a practical skill such as cloth, metal, stone, or woodworking. Most children were expected to learn the same skill as their parents; however, if a child desired another trade, he or she could go and temporarily live with a family in that trade. In addition to his/her trade, every citizen was responsible for growing food. Citizens worked for rotating two-year periods on the island's farms. These periods were staggered so that those in their second year trained the new arrivals. At harvest time, additional people would come from the cities to assist the farmers. As a result, crops could usually be harvested in a day or two, and there was abundant food for everyone. Utopians who needed anything (such as tools or supplies) simply went to a warehouse and requested the needed items free of charge. Only a few citizens (elected officials, scholars, diplomats, and priests) were excused from physical labor. With everyone working, and no one attempting to possess more than they actually needed, it was possible to limit the workday to six hours (this was written in a time where most people in the world worked from sunup to sundown). Non-working hours were devoted to education and the enjoyment of music and conversation. Practices such as gambling and hunting were disdained as wastes of time. Wasting time was always discouraged in a society in which "everyone has his eye on you, so you're practically forced to get on with your job, and make proper use of your spare time."

Because of the abundance of food, Hythloday reported that the Utopians enjoyed good health; however, there were also four hospitals in each city that dispensed free medical care to the sick. Priests counseled the incurably ill in euthanasia, but it was the individual's choice whether to shorten his/her pain through suicide or to continue living. Death was not considered a cause for mourning but rather as a time for joyous celebration of the individual's character and career. It was believed that the dead remained a presence within Utopia and constantly observed the activities of the community.

Crime was rare in Utopia because there was no incentive to steal in that all possessions belonged to everyone anyway. Doors of homes were always left unlocked because no one had any possessions to protect. Laws were so simply stated that lawyers were unnecessary, and those who were accused of breaking the laws could defend themselves if put on trial. The elected officials determined penalties for lawbreakers, and the most serious crimes were usually punished by the offender's being made a slave rather than being put to death. The death penalty was used only in cases of political conspiracy or repeated adultery.

Slavery was an important part of Utopian society. Slaves were either prisoners of war who had been captured by the Utopians, Utopians who were being punished for crimes, or refugees from other civilizations who gladly agreed to serve as slaves in order to live in Utopia. Slaves did farm work, hunted for food (a practice that Utopians were forbidden to participate in), and worked in the large dining halls where all Utopians ate their meals. Unlike later American slavery, Utopian slavery was not hereditary, and the children of slaves were not also considered to be slaves. Slaves, especially those who were being punished for crimes, could be freed from slavery by a pardon issued by the government.

Many religions were practiced in Utopia, from the worship of the sun or moon to a belief in one God. Utopians believed that divine truth would be eventually revealed in the afterlife, so it really did not matter if there were differences of opinion in regard to religion. The Utopians were receptive to Hythloday's explanations of Christianity but when a new convert to Christianity began to preach loudly in the streets, condemning other beliefs and attempting to convert others, he was banished from the community for disturbing the peace. In general, most religious beliefs were tolerated, although those who denied the existence of an afterlife with rewards or punishments for earthly behavior were denied the rights of citizenship on the grounds that those who did not believe in a final reckoning in the afterlife were more likely to violate the rules of the society. Utopians worshipped in large temples, with the men and women divided on opposite sides, and the children sitting in front of the women where they could be watched. Worship ceremonies were general in nature so as to accommodate various beliefs. Ceremonies which were peculiar to certain individual sects were performed privately. Worshippers dressed in plain white while the priests wore bright clothing decorated with the colorful feathers of birds. The people elected thirteen priests per city. Women could serve as priests but this was very rare and only older widows were ever chosen. In addition to spiritual duties, the priests were primarily responsible for the education of the young.

Utopians detested war but were willing to fight for good reasons; to defend themselves and their allies, deliver others from tyranny, or avenge their citizens who had been wronged by others. Their methods of warfare were unique. After war was declared, small numbers of Utopians would slip into enemy territory and post huge rewards for the capture or killing of the other country's top leaders. Enemies who betrayed their country were handsomely rewarded and protected. Many conflicts were won simply by causing dissension among Utopia's enemies. No Utopian was ever forced to serve in the military and they often hired mercenaries to do most of their fighting for them. Utopian soldiers who did choose to fight went into battle with their families right beside them to avoid the soldiers worrying about the condition of their loved ones at home and under the belief that they would fight harder to protect their loved ones if they were there with them. When victorious, the Utopians were generous conquerors, never putting prisoners to death, only demanding that their enemies pay for the cost of the war. Utopian soldiers were prohibited from taking any form of property from their enemies.

More described his purpose in writing *Utopia* as to offer a model of a society where man can live with his fellow man and find personal fulfillment without doing harm to others. He hoped that sixteenth century Europeans would use this novel as a basis of comparison to improve their own societies. Although his character Hythloday offered an extensive description of the "perfect" commonwealth, More was willing to argue many points with him, especially concerning the abolition of all personal property. *Utopia* was widely read and influenced centuries of writers as well as introducing the term "utopia" into the English language as a label for a perfect society.

THE FRENCH UTOPIANS

The French Revolution, with its call for "Liberty, Equality, and Fraternity," spawned many who would ponder the question of what constituted a perfect society. The lofty goals of the 1789 revolution soon transformed into disenchantment and bloodshed. The privileges (and even the lives) of the aristocracy were destroyed, but the society that replaced the old regime was even more tyrannical and bloodthirsty than its predecessor. It was the profound disappointment in the development of the revolution that led one of its strongest supporters, **François-Nöel Babeuf,** to form what became known as the Conspiracy of Equals in 1795. Babeuf argued that the revolution could not be complete until it rendered "true equality" for all. In his mind, this required the abolition of all private property and the dedication of the state to ensuring that all of the goods of society be shared equally. In a manifesto entitled *The Doctrine of Gracchus Babeuf,* he wrote: "In a real society there ought to be neither rich nor poor," and added that "the Aim of the French Revolution is to destroy inequality and to re-establish the general welfare." His other tenets included:

> Nature has bestowed upon each and every individual adequate right to the enjoyment of property.
>
> The purpose of society is to defend such equality, often assailed by the strong and the wicked in the state of nature, and to augment the general welfare through the co-operation of all.
>
> Nature has imposed upon each and every individual the obligation to work; anyone who evades his share of labor is a criminal.
>
> Both work and benefits must be common to all.
>
> There is oppression when one person is exhausted by labor and is destitute of everything, while another lives in luxury without doing any work at all.

> Anyone who appropriates exclusively to himself the products of the earth or of manufacture is a criminal.
>
> The rich who are not willing to renounce their surplus in favor of the poor are enemies of the people.
>
> No one, by accumulating to himself all power, may deprive another of the instruction necessary for his welfare. Education ought to be common to all.

Babeuf's contention that the revolution had been betrayed did not endear him to its rulers. He was arrested in 1796, carried to Paris in an iron cage, put on trial, and executed in May 1797. His idea that the goal of society should be to produce equality, however, later became the genesis (origin) of socialist and communist ideology.

A decade after Babeuf's execution, another Frenchman laid out extensive plans for an ideal society. **Charles Fourier** rejected the trend toward increasing urbanization and advocated that society needed to be reorganized into self-sufficient rural communities consisting of 1,620 persons. These communities, or phalanges, would seek to operate in harmony with nature and thereby eliminate all human conflict.[3] All work would be shared within the community. Fourier believed that modern society denied man's innate desire for variety. The unpleasantness of manual labor was primarily due to its repetitive nature; therefore, in his communities, workers would organize themselves into teams and rotate all jobs on an hourly basis. In his *Theory of Social Organization,* he also arrived at a solution to performing the society's most unattractive tasks:

> To secure the execution of uncleanly and offensive labors a body of youths—those attracted to much dirty work (youngsters aged nine to sixteen, composed of one-third girls, two-thirds boys)—what we shall call the Juvenile Legion—who shall perform them all. The young love to wade in the mire and play in dirt, are self-willed, rude, daring, and fond of gross language. From a sense of honor the Juvenile Legion will do the dirty jobs—highway repair, cleaning the stables, feeding and slaughtering animals, maintaining the buildings, and so forth.

Although he believed in free education for all, he believed that study in school should be regarded less important than the labor young people would perform in the community.

Fourier was strongly opposed to the institution of marriage, believing that it stifled the natural need for a variety of sexual partners and was in general harmful to the interests of women. An advocate of what would later be known as "women's liberation," Fourier believed that the level of any civilization could be determined by the extent to which its women had been liberated from traditional gender roles. He advocated that women have the same status as men and be permitted to choose as many partners as they desired, theorizing (in his typically precise manner) that most would prefer four.

Fourier's main ideas not only offended many, but the precision of his pronouncements and the bizarreness of some of his less essential predictions (such as that the seas would eventually lose their salt and become oceans of pink lemonade or that humans would eventually develop a third arm or *archibras*) often made him a target of ridicule. Undeterred, he worked endlessly to refine his plans and waited patiently for a rich benefactor to donate the money to put them into effect. Unfortunately for Fourier, this never occurred; however, after his death in 1837 others modified and publicized his ideas, giving rise to many planned communities based roughly upon his writings. During the 1840s, over 40 Fourier communities were established in the United States, the most famous being Brook Farm near Boston. Most lasted only a few years.

Claude Henri de Saint-Simon, an aristocratic Frenchman who had volunteered to fight in the American Revolution, was a contemporary of Fourier but took a very different view of organizing an ideal society. Rather than rejecting technological progress in favor of a simpler agrarian past, Saint-Simon embraced modernity. He believed that just as scientists were discovering that there were physical laws that dictated the operation of the natural world, a similar set of absolute laws governed the behavior of society. In the previous agricultural state, perhaps the landed aristocracy and religious authority of the church were needed to manage society, but in a modern state these were no longer necessary and should be replaced by a system in which intellectuals or scientists ruled for the benefit

[3]Fourier was obsessed with mathematical calculations. He arrived at 1,620 by determining that there existed exactly 810 differing psychological types or personalities. Allowing for one type of each sex, he determined the optimal number of 1,620. The term phalange came from the Greek battle formation, the phalanx, which grouped men tightly together in an interdependent and virtually impenetrable fighting unit.

of all. In his advocacy of a meritocracy (society based solely on one's achievements or qualifications), Saint-Simon advocated the abolition of individual inheritance rights, the public ownership of businesses, and gradual emancipation of women. Late in his life and after his death in 1825, numerous Saint-Simonien societies were established in France. Gradually, his followers became more radical, eventually calling for an end to all private property and wearing jackets that buttoned only in the back to stress the interdependence of mankind. They opened communal residences for the poor where they would share fellowship, meals, and child-care responsibilities. These residences were originally financed by donations from the wealthy; however, they were eventually supposed to be self-sufficient and supported by the wages of the residents. Most failed because they only attracted residents who were either unable or unwilling to find work.

NEW HARMONY

Utopian ideas were immensely popular in the United States during the first half of the nineteenth century. Three centuries after the publication of Sir Thomas More's *Utopia,* two attempts were made to establish Utopian settlements on the banks of the Wabash River in Southern Indiana. The first of these settlements was founded by a German religious leader, George Rapp, and the second by a British manufacturer, Robert Owen.

In the spring of 1814 over five hundred Germans, who had immigrated to America 11 years before, poled their boats up the Wabash into the young Indiana Territory to establish a settlement they called New Harmony. Their leader, George Rapp, was a large, 56-year-old man with a long flowing white beard. A successful farmer in Germany, Rapp had split from the Lutheran Church and attracted many followers to his belief that the second coming of Christ was imminent. He and his followers came to Pennsylvania in 1803 and established a settlement near Pittsburgh called Harmonie. This settlement was a resounding success, attracting an additional six hundred German settlers in its second year. The Rappites established several successful small industries in their community, including a whiskey distillery, in addition to profitably cultivating their 5,000-acre holdings. It was their inability, however, to grow grapes in the harsh Pennsylvania climate that motivated them to move west. Many of the men had been skilled winemakers in their native Germany, and even the economic success of their Pennsylvania settlement did not deter their strong desire to practice their craft in the New World. In testimony to the success of their Pennsylvania venture, after purchasing 25,000 acres of land in Indiana from the government for just over $61,000, the Rappites still left $12,000 on deposit in a Pittsburgh bank when they set out for Indiana.

Rapp and his followers devoutly believed that Christ's return to earth would come in their lifetime and were determined to purify themselves in anticipation of the great day. Seven years prior to their departure for Indiana, the group had adopted a policy of celibacy and most of the men and women in New Harmony were housed in separate dormitories. Some previously married Rappites chose to remain living together, but they were expected to abstain from sex. A Rappite schoolmaster later explained: "As they expect Christ to reappear soon, they wish to be prepared to meet him in a fit state, which they could not be if they were taken up by sensual pleasures." Nevertheless, a small number of children were born in the settlement despite this prohibition. In addition to celibacy, the Rappites also dispensed with private property. Settlers surrendered all their worldly goods and their personal share of any fruits of their labor in return for food, clothing, lodgings and "all such instruction in church and school as may be reasonably required." In 1818, they held a ceremony in which all records of the possessions that the settlers had originally brought with them to Indiana were burned.

Within ten years, New Harmony had developed into a resounding success. Compared to the haphazard manner in which most frontier towns grew, New Harmony seemed a genuine utopia to visitors with its neat rows of homes and fertile fields. Buildings were so solidly constructed that many remain today—four brick dormitories, each of them capable of housing sixty adults, complete with kitchens and community rooms; a large house for Rapp and his family; two granaries; a water mill and dam; a textile mill; a dye-house; two sawmills; a hemp and oil mill; two large distilleries; a brewery, in which the pump was operated by a large dog walking on a treadmill; forty two-story brick and frame homes; and eighty-six log homes, all with fences, stables, and gardens. The Rappites also constructed an elaborate labyrinth that symbolized man's struggle to negotiate the difficult path toward true harmony. $100,000 worth of goods per year flowed down the Wabash to the Ohio and on to New Orleans from the settlement. Farm crops, whiskey, wine, woolens, silks, wagons, hats, rope, and leatherworks were exported to 22 states and 10 foreign countries. Life in New Harmony was well ordered, beginning each morning with a call to work from French horns. Work stopped four times per day for meals: nine o'clock for lunch, noon for dinner, four o'clock for *vesperbrot,* and finally at sunset for dinner.

Due to geographic isolation and the policy of celibacy, the growth of the settlement soon stagnated. The close knit religious group did not seek new members nor worry much about the future due to their view that the world, as they knew it, was soon to end with the Second Coming. With little more to accomplish in Indiana and relations between the Rappite community and other settlers strained, Rapp decided to try to sell the settlement and move back east to Pennsylvania. He was astonished when, in 1824, his agent in Britain reported that he had quickly found a buyer willing to purchase the entire settlement for $130,000.

The purchaser of New Harmony was Robert Owen, a 53-year-old British textile manufacturer and social reformer. Owen had not only made a fortune in his business but also had transformed the dismal mill town of New Lanark, Scotland, into a world-renowned example of a model community. Owen believed "that the character of man is formed for him, not by him" and that "any character may be given to any community by the application of the proper means." In three decades at New Lanark, he had paid wages that afforded his workers a decent standard of living, and shortened the work day from thirteen to ten and a half hours in order to allow them the time and energy to improve their community. He also freed young children from the demands of daylong labor, establishing schools for them, including Britain's first efforts at early childhood education. Even more radical was his program that allowed the workers to share in the profits of the industry.

Although Owen's accomplishments at New Lanark were respected by many, his published attacks on organized religion, the negative effects of marriage on women, and the resentment of his fellow factory owners soon brought a strong wave of criticism from the British ruling classes. The opportunity to acquire land in America, where he could try out his social and economic views on a fresh canvas, proved irresistible to him, and he eagerly purchased New Harmony from George Rapp in January of 1825.

Owen immediately launched into his efforts to build a "New Moral World" on the banks of the Wabash. He gave two addresses to the United States Congress with the President and Supreme Court in attendance, outlining his plans, exhibiting drawings and models of his planned community, and predicting that communities like his would spread all over the United States. In response to his call, over 1,000 people descended on New Harmony even before the Rappites could vacate the town. In his first speech to the people of his settlement, Owen promised "to introduce an entire new state of society, to change it from an ignorant, selfish system to an enlightened social system which shall gradually unite all interests into one, and remove all contests between individuals." Owen's plans called for large rectangular settlements with public buildings located at the comers and workers' houses in between. The inner areas would be filled with botanical gardens and other recreational facilities. Education would be offered to all, with lessons adapted to the age and ability of the students. No one would own any property but all would share in the profit of the community. Owen initially appointed a temporary committee to rule but eventually all adults over the age of thirty would share the government.

Unfortunately, Owen was better at formulating plans than seeing them to their completion. After a brief stay in New Harmony, he left for seven months to publicize his "Community of Equality" and settle his business affairs in Scotland. During his absence, things began to fall apart. Many of the people who had been attracted by Owen's utopian dreams lacked the skill or inclination to build a successful community on the American frontier. Quarrels broke out over who would perform the necessary labor, and as a result, fields went unplanted and the settlers soon had to depend on purchasing food from other settlements.

In January of 1826, William Maclure joined Owen as partner in the venture. With him, Maclure brought a large group of intellectuals that Owen dubbed "The Boatload of Knowledge." Among this group were naturalists, schoolteachers, scientists, and writers. Although this small settlement on the frontier had one of the highest concentrations of intellect in all of America, it continued to flounder as the settlers read, debated, wrote, and attended lectures rather than performing the physical labor necessary for the settlement to survive.[4] As economic conditions worsened so did the atmosphere of cooperation that Owen so strongly hoped to instill. Many fights broke out. Two women had to be forcibly separated when they traded punches in the street in front of the community house. A group critical of Owen even went to the point of constructing a huge coffin to bury "Owenism" forever. Within two years, Owen was ready to admit defeat and move on to his next venture. He delivered farewell addresses in late May of 1827, deeded his property over to his sons, and left for Mexico to request (unsuccessfully) that the Mexican government give him Texas for his next experiment.

It is ironic that the Rappites, who intended their settlement only as a temporary waiting ground for the second coming, were much more successful than the Owenites, who were convinced that they were building a permanent settlement that would serve to inspire thousands of imitators. Many of the Rappite buildings still survive, while there are few physical reminders of Owen's settlement. George Rapp died at age 90, still believing that Christ would come in his lifetime, saying as he lay near death: "If I did not believe that the Lord intended me to present my people to Him on the last day, I would think I was dying." He left over half a million dollars in the vault of his great house from the successful efforts of his followers in Pennsylvania and Indiana. By 1905, only two of his followers remained, one of whom pronounced that the wait for the second coming was over and claimed the vast sum of the Rappites' wealth for himself. Robert Owen never succeeded in creating his "New View of Society," but his ideas became celebrated in the socialist philosophy of the British Labour Movement. His son, Robert Dale Owen, went on to serve two terms in the U.S. House of Representatives, representing the state of Indiana, and was instrumental in the creation of the Smithsonian Institution in Washington D.C.

THE SHAKERS

Although both of the New Harmony utopian communities had expired by 1830, another utopian movement in the United States was far more successful. The United Society of Believers in Christ, First and Second Appearing, was the nineteenth century's largest and best known communal society. The group, better known as Shakers due to their animated worship ceremonies, was founded in England by Ann Lee in the late eighteenth century and eventually established nineteen communities in America.

Ann Lee was born in Manchester, England, in 1736. Like most other poor Manchester girls, she began work in the textile mills before she was ten years old. The horrid conditions in the mills of Manchester had a profound effect on Lee as she witnessed firsthand all of the worst abuses of the still-young industrial revolution. Her marriage was an unhappy one, and all four of her children died in infancy. During the 1760s she began to be viewed as a spiritual leader within a small group of Manchester Quakers. Attempting to spread her beliefs, she was imprisoned in Manchester after she disrupted a Church of England worship ceremony. While imprisoned, Lee began to develop her religious beliefs into a coherent doctrine. Influenced perhaps by her unhappy marriage, Lee believed in the dissolution of all marriages and a life of celibacy. Her followers should separate themselves from the rest of the world, with all property held, not by individuals, but by the community as a whole.

Mother Ann, as she was known to her disciples, left England with a small number of followers in 1774 to begin a settlement in New York. The group established a small farming community near Albany, but was soon disrupted by the Revolutionary War. Committed pacifists, the Shakers refused to fight for either side in the war, and some of the men were jailed for refusing to join the Continental Army. Lee was also threatened with deportation, but the end of the war began an era of prosperity and growth for the Shakers as they were able to recruit numerous converts to their faith. Many of these converts were females, eager to avoid or escape the loneliness,

[4]Owen may have overlooked a key element in the success of New Lanark. His workforce was composed of a very homogeneous group of Scottish Calvinists, who believed that hard work was essential for salvation. The diverse group of settlers attracted to New Harmony did not share any common beliefs.

drudgery, and hard labor of being a farm wife. Despite the frequent separation of the genders, the Shakers believed in complete equality of the sexes. Every important position in the community was held both by a man and a woman.

Mother Ann died in 1784 at age 48, but her community continued to prosper. In 1805 the decision was made to expand the faith beyond the northeastern part of the country. Three colonizing missions were sent over the Appalachian Mountains; the largest of them arrived in Harrods Town, Kentucky, in August of 1805. Harrods Town (now Harrodsburg) had been established in 1774, the first permanent settlement in Kentucky. The Shakers settled nearby and named their 140-acre settlement Pleasant Hill.

The settlement soon became a huge economic success. It grew to encompass over 4,000 acres and housed 500 people at its peak. Sturdy buildings of limestone contained dormitories, mills, shops, and a laundry. The Shakers were prolific inventors, seeking to use technology to free up time for worship and contemplation. They developed an elaborate water pumping system powered by gravity with a huge wooden tank mounted on three stone pillars. The community grew wheat, rye, corn, flax, tobacco, and hemp (for rope). In addition, they raised cattle and sheep. In their shops, Shaker craftsmen produced their famous flat brooms, chairs, baskets, and cabinetry. Work began at four in the morning during the summer and at five in the winter. A clanging bell awakened the community in the morning and chores began only 15 minutes after the bell sounded. An hour and a half of work followed, and then the men and women assembled in two separate lines to await breakfast, which was eaten in silence. After breakfast, it was a return to work for five more hours prior to the day's main meal, which was consumed at noon. After eating, the community returned to work until six. The evening included a half hour of meditation followed by evening worship. The Sunday worship ceremonies began at ten in the morning as the men and women filed in through separate doors and took their seats on benches facing each other. During the ceremony, the two genders came into contact as they danced and sang together. In addition to Christmas, Mother Ann's birthday on February 29 or March 1 was celebrated as the birth of a second savior.

Throughout the first thirty years of its existence, the community continued to prosper and grow despite its policy of celibacy. In the beginning the growth was due to converts, drawn, no doubt, by the community's tranquility and economic success. The Shakers also began taking in orphans in 1833 after a cholera epidemic. This practice continued, especially during a second cholera epidemic in 1849. Kentucky was a slave state, and even though the Shakers disapproved of slavery, some converts brought their slaves with them to Pleasant Hill, where they were well treated. Some were eventually freed or purchased by the community. Several free Negroes were also members of the community at times.

The turmoil of the Civil War began the rapid decline of the Shaker community at Pleasant Hill. The war disrupted trade and threatened the economic well-being of the community. After the war, the rapid social and economic change of the post-war era made Pleasant Hill seem even further out of the mainstream than its founders had intended. Shaker support of the rights of the newly freed slaves brought retribution from the Ku Klux Klan. Several mysterious fires took place in the community, and an effort to recruit Swedish settlers proved divisive. The most significant problem, however, was simply that the community had aged, and the policy of celibacy had left it without a new generation of leadership. By 1884 the population had dropped below 200. Twelve years later, only sixty residents remained, and they were forced to sell some of the property to survive. Finally, in 1910, the remaining twelve inhabitants of the village deeded the remaining acres to a Harrodsburg resident in return for the promise that he would care for them until their death. Today only one active Shaker community still exists in America—Sabbathday, Maine.

In 1961 a nonprofit group was established to preserve the heritage of the Shaker Village at Pleasant Hill. Today 33 of the original buildings have been restored and 2,700 acres of farmland preserved. The Shaker Village is now a living museum, attracting thousands of visitors per year.

Harrison Bergeron

Kurt Vonnegut

The year was 2081, and everybody was finally equal. They weren't only equal before God and the law. They were equal every which way. Nobody was smarter than anybody else. Nobody was better looking than anybody else. Nobody was stronger or quicker than anybody else. All this equality was due to the 211th, 212th, and 213th Amendments to the Constitution, and to the unceasing vigilance of agents of the United States Handicapper General.

Some things about living still weren't quite right, though. April, for instance, still drove people crazy by not being springtime. And it was in that clammy month that the H-G men took George and Hazel Bergeron's fourteen-year-old son, Harrison, away.

It was tragic, all right, but George and Hazel couldn't think about it very hard. Hazel had a perfectly average intelligence, which meant she couldn't think about anything except in short bursts. And George, while his intelligence was way above normal, had a little mental handicap radio in his ear. He was required by law to wear it at all times. It was tuned to a government transmitter. Every twenty seconds or so, the transmitter would send out some sharp noise to keep people like George from taking unfair advantage of their brains.

George and Hazel were watching television. There were tears on Hazel's cheeks, but she'd forgotten for the moment what they were about.

On the television screen were ballerinas.

A buzzer sounded in George's head. His thoughts fled in panic, like bandits from a burglar alarm.

"That was a real pretty dance, that dance they just did," said Hazel.

"Huh?" said George.

"That dance—it was nice," said Hazel.

"Yup," said George. He tried to think a little about the ballerinas. They weren't really very good—no better than anybody else would have been, anyway. They were burdened with sash-weights and bags of birdshot, and their faces were masked, so that no one, seeing a free and graceful gesture or a pretty face, would feel like something the cat drug in. George was toying with the vague notion that maybe dancers shouldn't be handicapped. But he didn't get very far with it before another noise in his ear radio scattered his thoughts.

George winced. So did two out of the eight ballerinas.

Hazel saw him wince. Having no mental handicap herself, she had to ask George what the latest sound had been.

"Sounded like somebody hitting a milk bottle with a ball peen hammer," said George.

"I'd think it would be real interesting, hearing all the different sounds," said Hazel, a little envious. "All the things they think up."

"Um," said George.

"Only, if I was Handicapper General, you know what I would do?" said Hazel. Hazel, as a matter of fact, bore a strong resemblance to the Handicapper General, a woman named Diana Moon Glampers. "If I was Diana Moon Glampers," said Hazel, "I'd have chimes on Sunday—just chimes. Kind of in honor of religion."

"I could think, if it was just chimes," said George.

"Well—maybe make 'em real loud," said Hazel. "I think I'd make a good Handicapper General."

"Good as anybody else," said George.

"Who knows better'n I do what normal is?" said Hazel.

"Right," said George. He began to think glimmeringly about his abnormal son who was now in jail, about Harrison, but a twenty-one-gun salute in his head stopped that.

"Boy!" said Hazel, "that was a doozy, wasn't it?"

It was such a doozy that George was white and trembling, and tears stood on the rims of his red eyes. Two of the eight ballerinas had collapsed to the studio floor, were holding their temples.

"All of a sudden you look so tired," said Hazel. "Why don't you stretch out on the sofa, so's you can rest your handicap bag on the pillows, honeybunch." She was referring to the forty-seven pounds of birdshot in a canvas bag, which was padlocked around George's neck. "Go on and rest the bag for a little while," she said. "I don't care if you're not equal to me for a while."

George weighed the bag with his hands. "I don't mind it," he said. "I don't notice it any more. It's just a part of me."

"You been so tired lately—kind of wore out," said Hazel. "If there was just some way we could make a little hole in the bottom of the bag, and just take out a few of them lead balls. Just a few."

"Two years in prison and two thousand dollars fine for every ball I took out," said George. "I don't call that a bargain."

"If you could just take a few out when you came home from work," said Hazel. "I mean—you don't compete with anybody around here. You just set around."

"If I tried to get away with it," said George, "then other people'd get away with it—and pretty soon we'd be right back to the dark ages again, with everybody competing against everybody else. You wouldn't like that, would you?"

"I'd hate it," said Hazel.

"There you are," said George. "The minute people start cheating on laws, what do you think happens to society?"

If Hazel hadn't been able to come up with an answer to this question, George couldn't have supplied one. A siren was going off in his head.

"Reckon it'd fall all apart," said Hazel.

"What would?" said George blankly.

"Society," said Hazel uncertainly. "Wasn't that what you just said?"

"Who knows?" said George.

The television program was suddenly interrupted for a news bulletin. It wasn't clear at first as to what the bulletin was about, since the announcer, like all announcers, had a serious speech impediment. For about half a minute, and in a state of high excitement, the announcer tried to say, "Ladies and gentlemen—"

He finally gave up, handed the bulletin to a ballerina to read.

"That's all right—" Hazel said of the announcer, "he tried. That's the big thing. He tried to do the best he could with what God gave him. He should get a nice raise for trying so hard."

"Ladies and gentlemen—" said the ballerina, reading the bulletin. She must have been extraordinarily beautiful, because the mask she wore was hideous. And it was easy to see that she was the strongest and most graceful of all the dancers, for her handicap bags were as big as those worn by two-hundred-pound men.

And she had to apologize at once for her voice, which was a very unfair voice for a woman to use. Her voice was a warm, luminous, timeless melody. "Excuse me—" she said, and she began again, making her voice absolutely uncompetitive.

"Harrison Bergeron, age fourteen," she said in a grackle squawk, "has just escaped from jail, where he was held on suspicion of plotting to overthrow the government. He is a genius and an athlete, is under-handicapped, and should be regarded as extremely dangerous."

A police photograph of Harrison Bergeron was flashed on the screen-upside down, then sideways, upside down again, then right side up. The picture showed the full length of Harrison against a background calibrated in feet and inches. He was exactly seven feet tall.

The rest of Harrison's appearance was Halloween and hardware. Nobody had ever borne heavier handicaps. He had outgrown hindrances faster than the H-G men could think them up. Instead of a little ear radio for a mental handicap, he wore a tremendous pair of earphones, and spectacles with thick wavy lenses. The spectacles were intended to make him not only half blind, but to give him whanging headaches besides.

Scrap metal was hung all over him. Ordinarily, there was a certain symmetry, a military neatness to the handicaps issued to strong people, but Harrison looked like a walking junkyard. In the race of life, Harrison carried three hundred pounds.

And to offset his good looks, the H-G men required that he wear at all times a red rubber ball for a nose, keep his eyebrows shaved off, and cover his even white teeth with black caps at snaggle-tooth random.

"If you see this boy," said the ballerina, "do not—I repeat, do not—try to reason with him."

There was the shriek of a door being torn from its hinges.

Screams and barking cries of consternation came from the television set. The photograph of Harrison Bergeron on the screen jumped again and again, as though dancing to the tune of an earthquake.

George Bergeron correctly identified the earthquake, and well he might have—for many was the time his own home had danced to the same crashing tune. "My God—" said George, "that must be Harrison!"

The realization was blasted from his mind instantly by the sound of an automobile collision in his head.

When George could open his eyes again, the photograph of Harrison was gone. A living, breathing Harrison filled the screen.

Clanking, clownish, and huge, Harrison stood in the center of the studio. The knob of the uprooted studio door was still in his hand. Ballerinas, technicians, musicians, and announcers cowered on their knees before him, expecting to die.

"I am the Emperor!" cried Harrison. "Do you hear? I am the Emperor! Everybody must do what I say at once!" He stamped his foot and the studio shook.

"Even as I stand here—" he bellowed, "crippled, hobbled, sickened—I am a greater ruler than any man who ever lived! Now watch me become what I *can* become!"

Harrison tore the straps of his handicap harness like wet tissue paper, tore straps guaranteed to support five thousand pounds.

Harrison's scrap-iron handicaps crashed to the floor.

Harrison thrust his thumbs under the bar of the padlock that secured his head harness. The bar snapped like celery. Harrison smashed his headphones and spectacles against the wall.

He flung away his rubber-ball nose, revealed a man that would have awed Thor, the god of thunder.

"I shall now select my Empress!" he said, looking down on the cowering people. "Let the first woman who dares rise to her feet claim her mate and her throne!"

A moment passed, and then a ballerina arose, swaying like a willow.

Harrison plucked the mental handicap from her ear, snapped off her physical handicaps with marvellous delicacy. Last of all, he removed her mask.

She was blindingly beautiful.

"Now—" said Harrison, taking her hand, "shall we show the people the meaning of the word dance? Music!" he commanded.

The musicians scrambled back into their chairs, and Harrison stripped them of their handicaps, too. "Play your best," he told them, "and I'll make you barons and dukes and earls."

The music began. It was normal at first—cheap, silly, false. But Harrison snatched two musicians from their chairs, waved them like batons as he sang the music as he wanted it played. He slammed them back into their chairs.

The music began again and was much improved.

Harrison and his Empress merely listened to the music for a while—listened gravely, as though synchronizing their heartbeats with it.

They shifted their weights to their toes.

Harrison placed his big hands on the girl's tiny waist, letting her sense the weightlessness that would soon be hers.

And then, in an explosion of joy and grace, into the air they sprang!

Not only were the laws of the land abandoned, but the law of gravity and the laws of motion as well.

They reeled, whirled, swiveled, flounced, capered, gamboled, and spun.

They leaped like deer on the moon.

The studio ceiling was thirty feet high, but each leap brought the dancers nearer to it.

It became their obvious intention to kiss the ceiling.

They kissed it.

And then, neutralizing gravity with love and pure will, they remained suspended in air inches below the ceiling, and they kissed each other for a long, long time.

It was then that Diana Moon Glampers, the Handicapper General, came into the studio with a double-barreled ten-gauge shotgun. She fired twice, and the Emperor and the Empress were dead before they hit the floor.

Diana Moon Glampers loaded the gun again. She aimed it at the musicians and told them they had ten seconds to get their handicaps back on.

It was then that the Bergerons' television tube burned out.

Hazel turned to comment about the blackout to George. But George had gone out to the kitchen for a can of beer.

George came back in with the beer, paused while a handicap signal shook him up. And then he sat down again. "You been crying?" he said to Hazel.

"Yup," she said.

"What about?" he said.

"I forget," she said. "Something real sad on television."

"What was it?" he said,

"It's all kind of mixed up in my mind," said Hazel.

"Forget sad things," said George.

"I always do," said Hazel.

"That's my girl," said George. He winced. There was the sound of a riveting gun in his head.

"Gee—I could tell that one was a doozy," said Hazel.

"You can say that again," said George.

"Gee—" said Hazel, "I could tell that one was a doozy."

Trurl's Machine

Stanislaw Lem
translated bu Michael Kandel

Once upon a time Trurl the constructor built an eight-story thinking machine. When it was finished, he gave it a coat of white paint, trimmed the edges in lavender, stepped back, squinted, then added a little curlicue on the front and, where one might imagine the forehead to be, a few pale orange polka dots. Extremely pleased with himself, he whistled an air and, as is always done on such occasions, asked it the ritual question of how much is two plus two.

The machine stirred. Its tubes began to glow, its coils warmed up, current coursed through all its circuits like a waterfall, transformers hummed and throbbed, there was a clanging, and a chugging, and such an ungodly racket that Trurl began to think of adding a special mentation muffler. Meanwhile the machine labored on, as if it had been given the most difficult problem in the Universe to solve: the ground shook, the sand slid underfoot from the vibration, valves popped like champagne corks, the relays nearly gave way under the strain. At last, when Trurl had grown extremely impatient, the machine ground to a halt and said in a voice like thunder: SEVEN!

"Nonsense, my dear," said Trurl, "The answer's four. Now be a good machine and adjust yourself! What's two and two?" "SEVEN!" snapped the machine. Trurl sighed and put his coveralls back on, rolled up his sleeves, opened the bottom trapdoor and crawled in. For the longest time he hammered away inside, tightened, soldered, ran clattering up and down the metal stairs, now on the sixth floor, now on the eighth, then pounded back down to the bottom and threw a switch, but something sizzled in the middle, and the spark plugs grew blue whiskers. After two hours of this he came out, covered with soot but satisfied, put all his tools away, took off his coveralls, wiped his face and hands. As he was leaving, he turned and asked, just so there would be no doubt about it:

"And now what's two and two?"

"SEVEN!" replied the machine.

Trurl uttered a terrible oath, but there was no help for it—again he had to poke around inside the machine, disconnecting, correcting, checking, resetting, and when he learned for the third time that two and two was seven, he collapsed in despair at the foot of the machine, and sat there until Klapaucius found him. Klapaucius inquired what was wrong, for Trurl looked as if he had just returned from a funeral. Trurl explained the problem. Klapaucius crawled into the machine himself a couple of times, tried to fix this and that, then asked it for the sum of one plus two, which turned out to be six. One plus one, according to the machine, equaled zero. Klapaucius scratched his head, cleared his throat, and said:

"My friend, you'll just have to face it. That isn't the machine you wished to make. However, there's a good side to everything, including this."

"What good side?" muttered Trurl, and kicked the base on which he was sitting.

"Stop that," said the machine.

"H'm, it's sensitive too, But where was I? Oh yes . . . there's no question but that we have here a stupid machine, and not merely stupid in the usual, normal way, oh no! This is, as far as I can determine—and you know I am something of an expert—this is the stupidest thinking machine in the entire world, and that's nothing to sneeze at! To construct deliberately such a machine would be far from easy: in fact, I would say that no one could manage it. For the thing is not only stupid, but stubborn as a mule, that is, it has a personality common to idiots, for idiots are uncommonly stubborn."

"What earthly use do I have for such a machine?!" said Trurl, and kicked it again.

"I'm warning you, you better stop!" said the machine.

"A warning, if you please," observed Klapaucius dryly. "Not only is it sensitive, dense, and stubborn, but quick to take offense, and believe me, with such an abundance of qualities there are all sorts of things you might do!"

"What, for example?" asked Trurl.

"Well, it's hard to say offhand, You might put it on exhibit and charge admission; people would flock to see the stupidest thinking machine that ever was—what does it have, eight stories? Really, could anyone imagine a bigger dunce? And the exhibition would not only cover your costs, but—"

"Enough, I'm not holding any exhibition!" Trurl said, stood up, and, unable to restrain himself, kicked the machine once more.

"This is your third warning," said the machine.

"What?" cried Trurl, infuriated by its imperious manner. "You . . . you . . ." And he kicked it several times, shouting: "You're only good for kicking, you know that?"

"You have insulted me for the fourth, fifth, sixth, and eighth times," said the machine. "Therefore, I refuse to answer all further questions of a mathematical nature."

"It refuses! Do you hear that?" fumed Trurl, thoroughly exasperated. "After six comes eight—did you notice, Klapaucius?—not seven, but eight! And *that's* the kind of mathematics Her Highness refuses to perform! Take that! And that! And that! Or perhaps you'd like some more?"

The machine shuddered, shook, and without another word started to lift itself from its foundations. They were very deep, and the girders began to bend, but at last it scrambled out, leaving behind broken concrete blocks with steel spokes protruding—and it bore down on Trurl and Klapaucius like a moving fortress. Trurl was so dumbfounded that he didn't even try to hide from the machine, which to all appearances intended to crush him to a pulp. But Klapaucius grabbed his arm and yanked him away and the two of them took to their heels. When finally they looked back, they saw the machine swaying like a high tower, advancing slowly, at every step sinking to its second floor, but stubbornly, doggedly pulling itself out of the sand and heading straight for them.

"Whoever heard of such a thing?" Trurl gasped in amazement. "Why, this is mutiny! What do we do now?"

"Wait and watch," replied the prudent Klapaucius. "We may learn something."

But there was nothing to be learned just then. The machine had reached firmer ground and was picking up speed. Inside, it whistled, hissed, and sputtered,

"Any minute now the signal box will knock loose," said Trurl under his breath. "That'll jam the program and stop it. . . ."

"No," said Klapaucius, "this is a special case. The thing is so stupid, that even if the whole transmission goes, it won't matter. But—look out!!"

The machine was gathering momentum, clearly bent on running them down, so they fled just as fast as they could, the fearful rhythm of crunching steps in their ears. They ran and ran—what else could they do? They tried to make it back to their native district, but the machine outflanked them, cut them off, forced them deeper and deeper into a wild, uninhabited region. Mountains, dismal and craggy, slowly rose out of the mist. Trurl, panting heavily, shouted to Klapaucius:

"Listen! Let's turn into some narrow canyon . . . where it won't be able to follow us . . . the cursed thing . . . what do you say?"

"No . . . better go straight," wheezed Klapaucius. "There's a town up ahead . . . can't remember the name . . . anyway, we can find—oof!—find shelter there . . ."

So they ran straight and soon saw houses before them. The streets were practically deserted at this time of day, and the constructors had gone a good distance without meeting a living soul, when suddenly an awful crash, like an avalanche at the edge of the town, indicated that the machine was coming after them.

Trurl looked back and groaned.

"Good heavens! It's tearing down the houses, Klapaucius!!" For the machine, in stubborn pursuit, was plowing through the walls of the buildings like a mountain of steel, and in its wake lay piles of rubble and white clouds of plaster dust. There were dreadful screams, confusion in the streets, and Trurl and Klapaucius, their hearts in their mouths, ran on till they came to a large town hall, darted inside, and raced down endless stairs to a deep cellar.

"It won't get us in here, even if it brings the whole building down on our heads!" panted Klapaucius. "But really, the devil himself had me pay you a visit today. . . . I was curious to see how your work was going—well, I certainly found out. . . ."

"Quiet," interrupted Trurl. "Someone's coming. . . ."

And indeed, the cellar door opened up and the mayor entered, accompanied by several aldermen. Trurl was too embarrassed to explain how this strange and calamitous situation had come about: Klapaucius had to do it. The mayor listened in silence. Suddenly the walls trembled, the ground heaved, and the sound of cracking stone reached them in the cellar.

"It's here?!" cried Trurl.

"Yes," said the mayor. "And it demands that we give you up, otherwise it says it will level the entire town. . . ."

Just then they heard, far overhead, words that honked as if from a muffled horn:

"Trurl's here . . . I smell Trurl. . . ."

"But surely you won't give us up?" asked in a quavering voice the object of the machine's obstinate fury.

"The one of you who calls himself Trurl must leave. The other may remain, since surrendering him does not constitute part of the conditions. . . ."

"Have mercy!"

"We are helpless," said the mayor. "And were you to stay here, Trurl, you would have to answer for all the damage done to this town and its inhabitants, since it was because of you that the machine destroyed sixteen homes and buried beneath their ruins many of our finest citizens. Only the fact that you yourself stand in imminent peril permits me to let you leave unpunished. Go then, and nevermore return."

Trurl looked at the aldermen and, seeing his sentence written on their stern faces, slowly turned and made for the door,

"Wait! I'll go with you!" cried Klapaucius impulsively.

"You?" said Trurl, a faint hope in his voice. "But no . . ." he added after a moment. "Why should you have to perish too? . . ."

"Nonsense!" rejoined Klapaucius with great energy. "What, us perish at the hands that iron imbecile? Never! It takes more than that, my friend, to wipe two of the most famous constructors off the face of the globe! Come, Trurl! Chin up!"

Encouraged by these words, Trurl ran up the stairs after Klapaucius. There was not a soul outside in the square. Amid clouds of dust and the gaunt skeletons of demolished homes, stood the machine, higher than the town hall tower itself, puffing steam, covered with the blood of powdered brick and smeared with chalk.

"Careful!" whispered Klapaucius. "It doesn't see us. Let's take that first street on the left, then turn right, then straight for those mountains. There we can take refuge and think of how to make the thing give up once and for all its insane . . . *Now!*" he yelled, for the machine had just spotted them and was charging, making the pavement buckle.

Breathless, they ran from the town and galloped along for a mile or so, hearing behind them the thunderous stride of the colossus that followed relentlessly.

"I know that ravine!" Klapaucius suddenly cried. "That's the bed of a dried-out stream and it leads to cliffs and caves—faster, faster, the thing'll have to stop soon! . . ."

So they raced uphill, stumbling and waving their arms to keep their balance, but the machine still gained on them. Scrambling up over the gravel of the dried-out riverbed, they reached a crevice in the perpendicular rock and, seeing high above them the murky mouth of a cave, began to climb frantically toward it, no longer caring about the loose stones that flew from under their feet. The opening in the rock breathed chill and darkness. As quickly as they could, they leaped inside, ran a few extra steps, then stopped.

"Well, here at least we're safe," said Trurl, calm once again. "I'll just take a look, to see where it got stuck. . . ."

"Be careful," cautioned Klapaucius. Trurl inched his way to the edge of the cave, leaned out, and immediately jumped back in fright.

"It's coming up the mountain!!" he cried.

"Don't worry, it'll never be able to get in here," said Klapaucius, not altogether convinced. "But what's that? Is it getting dark? Oh no!"

At that moment a great shadow blotted out the bit of sky visible through the mouth of the cave, and in its place appeared a smooth steel wall with rows of rivets. It was the machine slowly closing with the rock, thereby sealing up the cave as if with a mighty metal lid.

"We're trapped . . ." whispered Trurl, his voice breaking off when the darkness became absolute.

"That was idiotic on our part!" Klapaucius exclaimed, furious. "To jump into a cave that it could barricade! How could we have done such a thing?"

"What do you think it's waiting for now?" asked Trurl after a long pause,

"For us to give up—that doesn't take any great brains."

Again there was silence. Trurl tiptoed in the darkness, hands outstretched, in the direction of the opening, running his fingers along the stone until he touched the smooth steel, which was warm, as if heated from within. . . .

"I feel Trurl . . ." boomed the iron voice. Trurl hastily retreated, took a seat alongside his friend, and for some time they sat there, motionless. At last Klapaucius whispered:

"There's no sense our just sitting here. I'll try to reason with it. . . ."

"That's hopeless," said Trurl. "But go ahead, Perhaps it will at least let *you* go free. . . ."

"Now, now, none of that!" said Klapaucius, patting him on the back, And he groped his way toward the mouth of the cave and called: "Hello out there, can you hear us?"

"Yes," said the machine.

"Listen, we'd like to apologize, You see . . . well, there was a little misunderstanding, true, but it was nothing, really. Trurl had no intention of . . ."

"I'll pulverize Trurl!" said the machine. "But first, he'll tell me how much two and two makes."

"Of course he will, of course he will, and you'll be happy with his answer, and make it up with him for sure, isn't that right, Trurl?" said the mediator soothingly,

"Yes, of course . . ." mumbled Trurl.

"Really?" said the machine. "Then how much is two and two?"

"Fo . . . that is, seven . . ." said Trurl in an even lower voice.

"Ha! Not four, but seven, eh?" crowed the machine. "There, I told you so!"

"Seven, yes, seven, we always knew it was seven!" Klapaucius eagerly agreed, "Now will you, uh, let us go?" he added cautiously.

"No, Let Trurl say how sorry he is and tell me how much is two times two. . . ."

"And you'll let us go, if I do?" asked Trurl.

"I don't know. I'll think about it. I'm not making any deals, What's two times two?"

"But you probably will let us go, won't you?" said Trurl, while Klapaucius pulled on his arm and hissed in his ear: "The thing's an imbecile, don't argue with it, for heaven's sake!"

"I won't let you go, if I don't want to," said the machine. "You just tell me how much two times two is. . . ."

Suddenly Trurl fell into a rage.

"I'll tell you, I'll tell you all right!" he screamed. "Two and two is four and two times two is four, even if you stand on your head, pound these mountains all to dust, drink the ocean dry, and swallow the sky—do you hear? Two and two is four!!"

"Trurl! What are you saying? Have you taken leave of your senses? Two and two is seven, nice machine! Seven, seven!!" howled Klapaucius, trying to drown out his friend,

"No! It's four! Four and only four, four from the beginning to the end of time—FOUR!!" bellowed Trurl growing hoarse.

The rock beneath their feet was seized with a feverish tremor,

The machine moved away from the cave, letting in a little pale light, and gave a piercing scream:

"That's not true! It's seven! Say it's seven or I'll hit you!"

"Never!" roared Trurl, as if he no longer cared what happened, and pebbles and dirt rained down on their heads, for the machine had begun to ram its eight-story hulk again and again into the wall of stone, hurling itself against the mountainside until huge boulders broke away and went tumbling down into the valley.

Thunder and sulfurous fumes filled the cave, and sparks flew from the blows of steel on rock, yet through all this pandemonium one could still make out, now and then, the ragged voice of Trurl bawling:

"Two and two is four! Two and two is four!!"

Klapaucius attempted to shut his friend's mouth by force, but, violently thrown off, he gave up, sat and covered his head with his arms. Not for a moment did the machine's mad efforts flag, and it seemed that any minute now the ceiling would collapse, crush the prisoners, and bury them forever. But when they had lost all hope, and the air was thick with acrid smoke and choking dust, there was suddenly a horrible scraping, and a sound like a slow explosion, louder than all the maniacal banging and battering, and the air whooshed, and the black wall that blocked the cave was whisked away, as if by a hurricane, and monstrous chunks of rock carne crashing down after it. The echoes of that avalanche still rumbled and reverberated in the valley below when the two friends peered out of their cave. They saw the machine. It lay smashed and flattened, nearly broken in half by an enormous boulder that had landed in the middle of its eight floors. With the greatest care they picked their way down through the smoking rubble. In order to reach the riverbed, it was necessary to pass the remains of the machine, which resembled the wreck of some mighty vessel thrown up upon a beach. Without a word, the two stopped together in the shadow of its twisted hull. The machine still quivered slightly, and one could hear something turning, creaking feebly, within.

"Yes, this is the bad end you've come to, and two and two is—as it always was—"began Trurl, but just then the machine made a faint, barely audible croaking noise and said, for the last time, "SEVEN."

Then something snapped inside, a few stones dribbled down from overhead, and now before them lay nothing but a lifeless mass of scrap. The two constructors exchanged a look and silently, without any further comment or conversation, walked back the way they came.

The Veldt

Ray Bradbury

"George, I wish you'd look at the nursery."

"What's wrong with it?"

"I don't know."

"Well, then."

"I just want you to look at it, is all, or call a psychologist in to look at it."

"What would a psychologist want with a nursery?"

"You know very well what he'd want." His wife paused in the middle of the kitchen and watched the stove busy humming to itself, making supper for four.

"It's just that the nursery is different now than it was."

"All right, let's have a look."

They walked down the hall of their soundproofed, Happy-life Home, which had cost them thirty thousand dollars installed, this house which clothed and fed and rocked them to sleep and played and sang and was good to them. Their approach sensitized a switch somewhere and the nursery light flicked on when they came within ten feet of it. Similarly, behind them, in the halls, lights went on and off as they left them behind, with a soft automaticity.

"Well," said George Hadley.

They stood on the thatched floor of the nursery. It was forty feet across by forty feet long and thirty feet high; it had cost half again as much as the rest of the house. "But nothing's too good for our children," George had said.

The nursery was silent. It was empty as a jungle glade at hot high noon. The walls were blank and two dimensional. Now, as George and Lydia Hadley stood in the center of the room, the walls began to purr and recede into crystalline distance, it seemed, and presently an African veldt appeared, in three dimensions; on all sides, in colors reproduced to the final pebble and bit of straw. The ceiling above them became a deep sky with a hot yellow sun.

George Hadley felt the perspiration start on his brow.

"Let's get out of the sun," he said. "This is a little too real. But I don't see anything wrong."

"Wait a moment, you'll see," said his wife.

Now the hidden odorophonics were beginning to blow a wind of odor at the two people in the middle of the baked veldtland. The hot straw smell of lion grass, the cool green smell of the hidden water hole, the great rusty smell of animals, the smell of dust like a red paprika in the hot air. And now the sounds: the thump of distant antelope feet on grassy sod, the papery rustling of vultures. A shadow passed through the sky. The shadow flickered on George Hadley's upturned, sweating face.

"Filthy creatures," he heard his wife say.

"The vultures."

"You see, there are the lions, far over, that way. Now they're on their way to the water hole. They've just been eating," said Lydia. "I don't know what."

"Some animal." George Hadley put his hand up to shield off the burning light from his squinted eyes. "A zebra or a baby giraffe, maybe."

"Are you sure?" His wife sounded peculiarly tense.

"No, it's a little late to be sure," he said, amused. "Nothing over there I can see but cleaned bone, and the vultures dropping for what's left."

"Did you hear that scream?" she asked.

"No."

"About a minute ago?"

"Sorry, no."

The lions were coming. And again George Hadley was filled with admiration for the mechanical genius who had conceived this room. A miracle of efficiency selling for an absurdly low price. Every home should have one. Oh, occasionally they frightened you with their clinical accuracy, they startled you, gave you a twinge, but most of the time what fun for everyone, not only your own son and daughter, but for yourself when you felt like a quick jaunt to a foreign land, a quick change of scenery. Well, here it was!

And here were the lions now, fifteen feet away, so real, so feverishly and startlingly real that you could feel the prickling fur on your hand, and your mouth was stuffed with the dusty upholstery smell of their heated pelts, and the yellow of them was in your eyes like the yellow of an exquisite French tapestry, the yellows of lions and summer grass, and the sound of the matted lion lungs exhaling on the silent noontide, and the smell of meat from the panting, dripping mouths.

The lions stood looking at George and Lydia Hadley with terrible green-yellow eyes.

"Watch out!" screamed Lydia.

The lions came running at them.

Lydia bolted and ran. Instinctively, George sprang after her. Outside, in the hall, with the door slammed, he was laughing and she was crying, and they both stood appalled at the other's reaction.

"George!"

"Lydia! Oh, my dear poor sweet Lydia!"

"They almost got us!"

"Walls, Lydia, remember; crystal walls, that's all they are. Oh, they look real, I must admit—Africa in your parlor—but it's all dimensional superractionary, supersensitive color film and mental tape film behind glass screens. It's all odorophonics and sonics, Lydia. Here's my handkerchief."

"I'm afraid." She came to him and put her body against him and cried steadily. "Did you see? Did you feel? It's too real."

"Now, Lydia..."

"You've got to tell Wendy and Peter not to read any more on Africa."

"Of course—of course." He patted her.

"Promise?"

"Sure."

"And lock the nursery for a few days until I get my nerves settled."

"You know how difficult Peter is about that. When I punished him a month ago by locking the nursery for even a few hours—the tantrum he threw! And Wendy too. They live for the nursery."

"It's got to be locked, that's all there is to it."

"All right." Reluctantly he locked the huge door. "You've been working too hard. You need a rest."

"I don't know—I don't know," she said, blowing her nose, sitting down in a chair that immediately began to rock and comfort her. "Maybe I don't have enough to do. Maybe I have time to think too much. Why don't we shut the whole house off for a few days and take a vacation?"

"You mean you want to fry my eggs for me?"

"Yes." She nodded.

"And darn my socks?"

"Yes." A frantic, watery-eyed nodding.

"And sweep the house?"

"Yes, yes—oh, yes!"

"But I thought that's why we bought this house, so we wouldn't have to do anything?"

"That's just it. I feel like I don't belong here. The house is wife and mother now and nursemaid. Can I compete with an African veldt? Can I give a bath and scrub the children as efficiently or quickly as the automatic scrub bath can? I cannot. And it isn't just me. It's you. You've been awfully nervous lately."

"I suppose I have been smoking too much."

"You look as if you didn't know what to do with yourself in this house, either. You smoke a little more every morning and drink a little more every afternoon and need a little more sedative every night. You're beginning to feel unnecessary too."

"Am I?" He paused and tried to feel into himself to see what was really there.

"Oh, George!" She looked beyond him, at the nursery door. "Those lions can't get out of there, can they?"

He looked at the door and saw it tremble as if something had jumped against it from the other side.

"Of course not," he said.

At dinner they ate alone, for Wendy and Peter were at a special plastic carnival across town and had televised home to say they'd be late, to go ahead eating. So George Hadley, bemused, sat watching the dining-room table produce warm dishes of food from its mechanical interior.

"We forgot the ketchup," he said.

"Sorry," said a small voice within the table, and ketchup appeared.

As for the nursery, thought George Hadley, it won't hurt for the children to be locked out of it awhile. Too much of anything isn't good for anyone. And it was clearly indicated that the children had been spending a little too much time on Africa. That *sun*. He could feel it on his neck, still, like a hot paw. And the *lions*. And the smell of blood. Remarkable how the nursery caught the telepathic emanations of the children's minds and created life to fill their every desire. The children thought lions, and there were lions. The children thought zebras, and there were zebras. Sun—sun. Giraffes—giraffes. Death and death.

That last. He chewed tastelessly on the meat that the table had cut for him. Death thoughts. They were awfully young, Wendy and Peter, for death thoughts. Or, no, you were never too young, really. Long before you knew what death was you were wishing it on someone else. When you were two years old you were shooting people with cap pistols.

But this—the long, hot African veldt—the awful death in the jaws of a lion. And repeated again and again.

"Where are you going?"

He didn't answer Lydia. Preoccupied, he let the lights glow softly on ahead of him, extinguish behind him as he padded to the nursery door. He listened against it. Far away, a lion roared.

He unlocked the door and opened it. Just before he stepped inside, he heard a faraway scream. And then another roar from the lions, which subsided quickly.

He stepped into Africa. How many times in the last year had he opened this door and found Wonderland, Alice, the Mock Turtle, or Aladdin and his Magical Lamp, or Jack Pumpkinhead of Oz, or Dr. Doolittle, or the cow jumping over a very real-appearing moon—all the delightful contraptions of a make-believe world. How often had he seen Pegasus flying in the sky ceiling, or seen fountains of red fireworks, or heard angel voices singing. But now, this yellow hot Africa, this bake oven with murder in the heat. Perhaps Lydia was right. Perhaps they needed a little vacation from the fantasy which was growing a bit too real for ten-year-old children. It was all right to exercise one's mind with gymnastic fantasies, but when the lively child mind settled on one pattern . . .? It seemed that at a distance, for the past month, he had heard lions roaring, and smelled their strong odor seeping as far away as his study door. But, being busy, he had paid it no attention.

George Hadley stood on the African grassland alone. The lions looked up from their feeding, watching him. The only flaw to the illusion was the open door through which he could see his wife, far down the dark hall, like a framed picture, eating her dinner abstractedly.

"Go away," he said to the lions.

They did not go.

He knew the principle of the room exactly. You sent out your thoughts. Whatever you thought would appear.

"Let's have Aladdin and his lamp," he snapped. The veldtland remained; the lions remained.

"Come on, room! I demand Aladdin!" he said.

Nothing happened. The lions mumbled in their baked pelts.

"Aladdin!"

He went back to dinner. "The fool room's out of order," he said. "It won't respond."

"Or—"

"Or what?"

"Or it *can't* respond," said Lydia, "because the children have thought about Africa and lions and killing so many days that the room's in a rut."

"Could be."

"Or Peter's set it to remain that way."

"Set it?"

"He may have got into the machinery and fixed something."

"Peter doesn't know machinery."

"He's a wise one for ten. That I.Q. of his—"

"Nevertheless—"

"Hello, Mom. Hello, Dad."

The Hadleys turned. Wendy and Peter were coming in the front door, cheeks like peppermint candy, eyes like bright blue agate marbles, a smell of ozone on their jumpers from their trip in the helicopter.

"You're just in time for supper," said both parents.

"We're full of strawberry ice cream and hot dogs," said the children, holding hands. "But we'll sit and watch."

"Yes, come tell us about the nursery," said George Hadley. The brother and sister blinked at him and then at each other. "Nursery?"

"All about Africa and everything," said the father with false joviality.

"I don't understand," said Peter.

"Your mother and I were just traveling through Africa with rod and reel; Tom Swift and his Electric Lion," said George Hadley.

"There's no Africa in the nursery," said Peter simply.

"Oh come now, Peter. We know better."

"I don't remember any Africa," said Peter to Wendy. "Do you?"

"No."

"Run see and come tell."

She obeyed.

"Wendy, come back here!" said George Hadley, but she was gone. The house lights followed her like a flock of fireflies. Too late, he realized he had forgotten to lock the nursery door after his last inspection.

"Wendy'll look and come tell us," said Peter.

"She doesn't have to tell me. I've seen it."

"I'm sure you're mistaken, Father."

"I'm not, Peter. Come along now."

But Wendy was back. "It's not Africa," she said breathlessly.

"We'll see about this," said George Hadley, and they all walked down the hall together and opened the nursery door.

There was a green, lovely forest, a lovely river, a purple mountain, high voices singing, and Rima, lovely and mysterious, lurking in the trees with colorful flights of butterflies, like animated bouquets, lingering in her long hair. The African veldtland was gone. The lions were gone. Only Rima was here now, singing a song so beautiful that it brought tears to your eyes.

George Hadley looked in at the changed scene. "Go to bed," he said to the children.

They opened their mouths.

"You heard me," he said.

They went off to the air closet, where a wind sucked them like brown leaves up the flue to their slumber rooms.

George Hadley walked through the singing glade and picked up something that lay in the corner near where the lions had been. He walked slowly back to his wife.

"What is that?" she asked.

"An old wallet of mine," he said.

He showed it to her. The smell of hot grass was on it and the smell of a lion. There were drops of saliva on it, it had been chewed, and there were blood smears on both sides.

He closed the nursery door and locked it, tight.

In the middle of the night he was still awake and he knew his wife was awake. "Do you think Wendy changed it?" she said at last, in the dark room.

"Of course."

"Made it from a veldt into a forest and put Rima there instead of lions?"

"Yes."

"Why?"

"I don't know. But it's staying locked until I find out."

"How did your wallet get there?"

"I don't know anything," he said, "except that I'm beginning to be sorry we bought that room for the children. If children are neurotic at all, a room like that—"

"It's supposed to help them work off their neuroses in a healthful way."

"I'm starting to wonder." He stared at the ceiling.

"We've given the children everything they ever wanted. Is this our reward—secrecy, disobedience?"

"Who was it said, 'Children are carpets, they should be stepped on occasionally'? We've never lifted a hand. They're insufferable—let's admit it. They come and go when they like; they treat us as if we were offspring. They're spoiled and we're spoiled."

"They've been acting funny ever since you forbade them to take the rocket to New York a few months ago."

"They're not old enough to do that alone, I explained."

"Nevertheless, I've noticed they've been decidedly cool toward us since."

"I think I'll have David McClean come tomorrow morning to have a look at Africa."

"But it's not Africa now, it's Green Mansions country and Rima."

"I have a feeling it'll be Africa again before then."

A moment later they heard the screams. Two screams. Two people screaming from downstairs. And then a roar of lions.

"Wendy and Peter aren't in their rooms," said his wife.

He lay in his bed with his beating heart. "No," he said. "They've broken into the nursery."

"Those screams—they sound familiar."

"Do they?"

"Yes, awfully."

And although their beds tried very hard, the two adults couldn't be rocked to sleep for another hour. A smell of cats was in the night air.

"Father?" said Peter.

"Yes."

Peter looked at his shoes. He never looked at his father any more, nor at his mother. "You aren't going to lock up the nursery for good, are you?"

"That all depends."

"On what?" snapped Peter.

"On you and your sister. If you intersperse this Africa with a little variety—oh, Sweden perhaps, or Denmark or China—"

"I thought we were free to play as we wished."

"You are, within reasonable bounds."

"What's wrong with Africa, Father?"

"Oh, so now you admit you have been conjuring up Africa, do you?"

"I wouldn't want the nursery locked up," said Peter coldly. "Ever."

"Matter of fact, we're thinking of turning the whole house off for about a month. Live sort of a carefree one-for-all existence."

"That sounds dreadful! Would I have to tie my own shoes instead of letting the shoe tier do it? And brush my own teeth and comb my hair and give myself a bath?"

"It would be fun for a change, don't you think?"

"No, it would be horrid. I didn't like it when you took out the picture painter last month."

"That's because I wanted you to learn to paint all by yourself, son."

"I don't want to do anything but look and listen and smell; what else *is* there to do?"

"All right, go play in Africa."

"Will you shut off the house sometime soon?"

"We're considering it."

"I don't think you'd better consider it any more, Father."

"I won't have any threats from my son!"

"Very well." And Peter strolled off to the nursery.

"Am I on time?" said David McClean.

"Breakfast?" asked George Hadley.

"Thanks, had some. What's the trouble?"

"David, you're a psychologist."

"I should hope so."

"Well, then, have a look at our nursery. You saw it a year ago when you dropped by; did you notice anything peculiar about it then?"

"Can't say I did; the usual violences, a tendency toward a slight paranoia here or there, usual in children because they feel persecuted by parents constantly, but, oh, really nothing."

They walked down the hall. "I locked the nursery up," explained the father, "and the children broke back into it during the night. I let them stay so they could form the patterns for you to see."

There was a terrible screaming from the nursery.

"There it is," said George Hadley. "See what you make of it."

They walked in on the children without rapping.

The screams had faded. The lions were feeding.

"Run outside a moment, children," said George Hadley. "No, don't change the mental combination. Leave the walls as they are. Get!"

With the children gone, the two men stood studying the lions clustered at a distance, eating with great relish whatever it was they had caught.

"I wish I knew what it was," said George Hadley. "Sometimes I can almost see. Do you think if I brought high-powered binoculars here and—"

David McClean laughed dryly. "Hardly." He turned to study all four walls. "How long has this been going on?"

"A little over a month."

"It certainly doesn't *feel* good."

"I want facts, not feelings."

"My dear George, a psychologist never saw a fact in his life. He only hears about feelings; vague things. This doesn't feel good, I tell you. Trust my hunches and my instincts. I have a nose for something bad. This is very bad. My advice to you is to have the whole damn room torn down and your children brought to me every day during the next year for treatment."

"Is it that bad?"

"I'm afraid so. One of the original uses of these nurseries was so that we could study the patterns left on the walls by the child's mind, study at our leisure, and help the child. In this case, however, the room has become a channel toward destructive thoughts, instead of a release away from them."

"Didn't you sense this before?"

"I sensed only that you had spoiled your children more than most. And now you're letting them down in some way. What way?"

"I wouldn't let them go to New York."

"What else?"

"I've taken a few machines from the house and threatened them, a month ago, with closing up the nursery unless they did their homework. I did close it for a few days to show I meant business."

"Ah, ha!"

"Does that mean anything?"

"Everything. Where before they had a Santa Claus now they have a Scrooge. Children prefer Santas. You've let this room and this house replace you and your wife in your children's affections. This room is their mother and father, far more important in their lives than their real parents. And now you come along and want to shut it off. No wonder there's hatred here. You can feel it coming out of the sky. Feel that sun. George, you'll have to change your life. Like too many others, you've built it around creature comforts. Why, you'd starve tomorrow if something went wrong in your kitchen. You wouldn't know how to tap an egg. Nevertheless, turn everything off. Start new. It'll take time. But we'll make good children out of bad in a year, wait and see."

"But won't the shock be too much for the children, shutting the room up abruptly, for good?"

"I don't want them going any deeper into this, that's all."

The lions were finished with their red feast.

The lions were standing on the edge of the clearing watching the two men.

"Now *I'm* feeling persecuted," said McClean. "Let's get out of here. I never have cared for these damned rooms. Make me nervous."

"The lions look real, don't they?" said George Hadley. "I don't suppose there's any way—"

"What?"

"—that they could become real?"

"Not that I know."

"Some flaw in the machinery, a tampering or something?"

"No."

They went to the door.

"I don't imagine the room will like being turned off," said the father.

"Nothing ever likes to die—even a room."

"I wonder if it hates me for wanting to switch it off?"

"Paranoia is thick around here today," said David McClean. "You can follow it like a spoor. Hello." He bent and picked up a bloody scarf.

"This ours?"

"No." George Hadley's face was rigid. "It belongs to Lydia."

They went to the fuse box together and threw the switch that killed the nursery.

The two children were in hysterics. They screamed and pranced and threw things. They yelled and sobbed and swore and jumped at the furniture.

"You can't do that to the nursery, you can't!"

"Now, children."

The children flung themselves onto a couch, weeping.

"George," said Lydia Hadley, "turn on the nursery, just for a few moments. You can't be so abrupt."

"No."

"You can't be so cruel."

"Lydia, it's off, and it stays off. And the whole damn house dies as of here and now. The more I see of the mess we've put ourselves in, the more it sickens me. We've been contemplating our mechanical, electronic navels for too long. My God, how we need a breath of honest air!"

And he marched about the house turning off the voice clocks, the stoves, the heaters, the shoe shiners, the shoe lacers, the body scrubbers and swabbers and massagers, and every other machine he could put his hand to.

The house was full of dead bodies, it seemed. It felt like a mechanical cemetery. So silent. None of the humming hidden energy of machines waiting to function at the tap of a button.

"Don't let them do it!" wailed Peter at the ceiling, as if he was talking to the house, the nursery. "Don't let Father kill everything." He turned to his father. "Oh, I hate you!"

"Insults won't get you anywhere."

"I wish you were dead!"

"We were, for a long while. Now we're going to really start living. Instead of being handled and massaged, we're going to *live*."

Wendy was still crying and Peter joined her again. "Just a moment, just one moment, just another moment of nursery," they wailed.

"Oh, George," said the wife, "it can't hurt."

"All right—all right, if they'll only just shut up. One minute, mind you, and then off forever."

"Daddy, Daddy, Daddy!" sang the children, smiling with wet faces.

"And then we're going on a vacation. David McClean is coming back in half an hour to help us move out and get to the airport. I'm going to dress. You turn the nursery on for a minute, Lydia, just a minute, mind you."

And the three of them went babbling off while he let himself be vacuumed upstairs through the air flue and set about dressing himself. A minute later Lydia appeared.

"I'll be glad when we get away," she sighed.

"Did you leave them in the nursery?"

"I wanted to dress too. Oh, that horrid Africa. What can they see in it?"

"Well, in five minutes we'll be on our way to Iowa. Lord, how did we ever get in this house? What prompted us to buy a nightmare?"

"Pride, money, foolishness."

"I think we'd better get downstairs before those kids get engrossed with those damned beasts again."

Just then they heard the children calling, "Daddy, Mommy, come quick—quick!"

They went downstairs in the air flue and ran down the hall. The children were nowhere in sight. "Wendy? Peter!"

They ran into the nursery. The veldtland was empty save for the lions waiting, looking at them. "Peter, Wendy?"

The door slammed.

"Wendy, Peter!"

George Hadley and his wife whirled and ran back to the door.

"Open the door!" cried George Hadley, trying the knob. "Why, they've locked it from the outside! Peter!" He beat at the door. "Open up!"

He heard Peter's voice outside, against the door. "Don't let them switch off the nursery and the house," he was saying.

Mr. and Mrs. George Hadley beat at the door. "Now, don't be ridiculous, children. It's time to go. Mr. McClean'll be here in a minute and . . ."

And then they heard the sounds.

The lions on three sides of them, in the yellow veldt grass, padding through the dry straw, rumbling and roaring in their throats.

The lions.

Mr. Hadley looked at his wife and they turned and looked back at the beasts edging slowly forward, crouching, tails stiff.

Mr. and Mrs. Hadley screamed.

And suddenly they realized why those other screams had sounded familiar.

"Well, here I am," said David McClean in the nursery doorway. "Oh, hello." He stared at the two children seated in the center of the open glade eating a little picnic lunch. Beyond them was the water hole and the yellow veldtland; above was the hot sun. He began to perspire. "Where are your father and mother?"

The children looked up and smiled. "Oh, they'll be here directly."

"Good, we must get going." At a distance Mr. McClean saw the lions fighting and clawing and then quieting down to feed in silence under the shady trees.

He squinted at the lions with his hand up to his eyes.

Now the lions were done feeding. They moved to the water hole to drink.

A shadow flickered over Mr. McClean's hot face. Many shadows flickered. The vultures were dropping down the blazing sky.

"A cup of tea?" asked Wendy in the silence.

The Unicorn Man of India

James Cross Giblin

The unicorn of India resembled neither a wild ass nor a rhinoceros. This unicorn wasn't even an animal; it was a handsome young man named Risharinga.

Risharinga first appeared in the pages of an Indian epic, *The Mahabharata,* that was written about 200 B.C. *Mahabharata* means "great story" in the Sanskrit language, and the book was a combination of myths and history. Many of the stories in it, including the one about the unicorn man, had been told and retold in India for hundreds of years before they were finally written down.

According to *The Mahabharata,* Risharinga's father was a Hindu holy man, Kasyapa. Tired of the world, Kasyapa decided to go off by himself and lead a life of poverty and meditation.

"Let him wander alone like a rhinoceros horn," said Kasyapa's friends. Their words were meant to be an encouragement to him. Since horns usually came in pairs, Kasyapa would be even more self-sufficient—and more religious—if he were like the single horn of the Indian rhinoceros, which, they believed, had the strength of two.

After journeying through a deep forest, Kasyapa came to the banks of the holy River Kausiki. There he built a hut for himself, and for many years he lived alone in it. When he was hungry, he went into the forest to gather wild fruits and nuts. Otherwise, he spent his days and nights in meditation.

One evening, just before sunset, a beautiful doe antelope appeared on the bank of the river near Kasyapa's hut. She seemed to be surrounded by a golden glow, and Kasyapa was captivated by her beauty. He approached her slowly, fearing she might turn and run away, but her eyes never left his.

The doe stayed with Kasyapa, and some months later she gave birth to a handsome baby son. He was formed like a human in all respects but one: From the middle of his forehead grew a single horn curved like those of the male antelope.

Shortly after the baby was born, the doe became ill. She developed a high fever and within a few days she died, despite all of Kasyapa's attempts to save her. The grief-stricken man was left to raise their son by himself. He named the boy Risharinga, meaning "antelope horn," and the child grew up never knowing any other human except his father.

When Risharinga was a young man, the land was ruled by an arrogant king named Lomapada. King Lomapada refused to listen to the advice of his priests and wise men and thought only of himself and his own pleasures. He amassed great wealth while his people went hungry.

As a result of the king's selfish actions, the gods became angry and caused all rains to stop. A terrible drought struck the land. The crops turned brown and died, and when King Lomapada sent out his stewards to obtain provisions for the palace, they came back empty-handed.

In despair, the king turned to his priests and wise men and asked them what he should do. One said: "Send for Risharinga, the hermit's son, the one with a horn growing out of his forehead. He is a forest child, ignorant of the ways of the world, and devoted to uprightness. If he comes to your kingdom, the gods will relent and cause heavy rains to fall once more."

"How will I persuade Risharinga to come?" asked the king.

"Send your daughter, Shanta, up the River Kausiki in a boat laden with flowers and fruit," said the wise man. "Risharinga has never seen a woman, and he will be charmed by her."

"But Shanta is my only child!" protested the king. "How can I send her on such a mission?"

"Only a beautiful maiden like Shanta will be successful," said the wise man, and at last the king was convinced. A magnificent boat was stocked with every luxury, and Shanta set sail up the river in search of Risharinga. The girl was fearful, but she knew the lives of her people and her country were at stake.

As the boat neared the spot where Risharinga lived, the princess saw a young man picking berries from a patch of bushes on the riverbank. He was a tall, handsome youth dressed in the simple clothes of a hermit. But the curving horn that grew from his forehead marked him as Risharinga. The princess ordered the sailors to moor the boat, and she stepped gracefully ashore.

When Risharinga looked up and saw Shanta, he was struck by her beauty as his father had been struck by the beauty of the doe. He offered her berries from his basket, and the princess took a handful. She, in turn, offered him fruit from the boat, and a cool, delicious drink.

After they had finished eating, the princess got a ball from the boat and tossed it to Risharinga. For a moment he was confused; he had never played with a ball before. Then he tossed it back to Shanta.

She plucked flowers from a vine and twined them around Risharinga's horn. By now she had become used to the horn, and even found it attractive. She stood on tiptoe to give Risharinga a kiss. Then she stepped aboard her boat and sailed back the way she had come.

Risharinga went home able to think of nothing but the beautiful princess. When his father returned to the hut from gathering wild fruit in the forest, he told him all about Shanga.

Kasyapa was furious, and called her a temptress. He forbade Risharinga to see her again and made the youth promise to expel all thoughts of her from his mind. But Risharinga could not. He lay awake that night, seeing again Shanta's face and the silken garments she wore, and hearing her laugh as she tossed the ball to him.

When his father went off into the forest the next day to gather more fruit, Risharinga waited until he was out of sight and then hurried along the riverbank in search of Shanta. A few miles downriver, he found her boat at anchor. She was overjoyed to see him and invited him aboard the boat. They sailed away together before Risharinga's father could return and prevent his son from going.

As they neared her kingdom, Risharinga told the princess how much he loved her. She, in turn, confessed why she had sought him out in the first place. He was upset and angry until she took his hands and assured him that she loved him as much as he loved her.

Then Shanta pointed out the terrible sights to be seen on both sides of the river—the dried-up farmyards, the abandoned houses, the animals lying dead in the fields. Gazing at all the devastation, Risharinga wept tears of sorrow and compassion. At that very moment, a hard, soaking rain began to fall, just as the wise man had predicted.

When Risharinga and Shanta arrived at the palace, her father, the king, was startled at first. He had never seen anything like the single horn that grew out of the young man's forehead. But then the king remembered the good deed Risharinga had performed. He announced to everyone present that he would give his daughter in marriage to the unicorn man in gratitude for his having saved the country.

Hearing the king's words, Risharinga and the princess clasped hands delightedly.

The king also announced that when Risharinga's father came in search of his son, he should be told that all the cows and crops in the rain-refreshed fields were Risharinga's. And the unicorn man could dispense this wealth in any charitable way he wished.

This was done, and Kasyapa's anger had cooled by the time he reached the palace. There he joined in the wedding celebrations for Risharinga and the princess, and they all lived happily from that time onward.

* * *

The gentle unicorn man provided a fine example of Hindu religious ideals in action. We may wonder how Risharinga's mother could be a doe antelope, but Hindu readers and listeners would have understood that she was a divine maiden who had been put under a curse by evil spirits. Such transformations happen frequently in Hindu literature, just as they do in European fairy tales. Hindus would also have recognized that Risharinga's horn symbolized the divine qualities of sensitivity and compassion that he had inherited from his mother.

Barbie-Q

Sandra Cisneros

Yours is the one with mean eyes and a ponytail. Striped swimsuit, stilettos, sunglasses, and gold hoop earrings. Mine is the one with bubble hair. Red swimsuit, stilettos, pearl earrings, and a wire stand. But that's all we can afford, besides one extra outfit apiece. Yours, "Red Flair," sophisticated A-line coatdress with a Jackie Kennedy pillbox hat, white gloves, handbag, and heels included. Mine, "Solo in the Spotlight," evening elegance in black glitter strapless gown with a puffy skirt at the bottom like a mermaid tail, formal length gloves, pink chiffon scarf, and mike included. From so much dressing and undressing, the black glitter wears off where her titties stick out. This and a dress invented from an old sock where we cut holes here and here and here, the cuff rolled over for the glamorous, fancy-free, off-the-shoulder look.

Every time the same story. Your Barbie is roommates with my Barbie, and my Barbie's boyfriend comes over and your Barbie steals him, okay? Kiss kiss kiss. Then the two Barbies fight. You dumbbell! He's mine. On no he's not, you stinky! Only Ken's invisible, right? Because we don't have money for a stupid-looking boy doll when we'd both rather ask for a new Barbie outfit next Christmas. We have to make do with your mean-eyed Barbie and my bubblehead Barbie and our one outfit apiece not including the sock dress.

Until next Sunday when we are walking through the flea market on Maxwell Street and *there!* Lying on the street next to some tool bits, and platform shoes with the heels all squashed, and a fluorescent green wicker wastebasket, and aluminum foil, and hubcaps, and a pink shag rug, and windshield wiper blades, and dusty mason jars, and a coffee can full of rusty nails. *There!* Where? Two Mattel boxes. One with the "Career Gal" ensemble, snappy black-and-white business suit, three-quarter-length sleeve jacket with kick-pleat skirt, red sleeveless shell, gloves, pumps, and matching hat included. The other, "Sweet Dreams," dreamy pink-and-white plaid nightgown and matching robe, lace-trimmed slippers, hairbrush and hand mirror included. How much? Please, please, please, please, please, please, please, until they say okay.

On the outside you and me skipping and humming but inside we are doing loopity-loops and pirouetting. Until at the next vendor's stand, next to boxed pies, and bright orange toilet brushes, and rubber gloves, and wrench sets, and bouquets of feather flowers, and glass towel racks, and steel wool, and Alvin and the Chipmunks records, *there!* And *there!* And *there!* And *there!* and *there!* and *there!* and *there!* Bendable Legs Barbie with her new page-boy hairdo. Midge, Barbie's best friend. Ken, Barbie's boyfriend. Skipper, Barbie's little sister. Tutti and Todd, Barbie and Skipper's tiny twin sister and brother. Skipper's friends, Scooter and Ricky. Alan, Ken's buddy. And Francie, Barbie's MOD'ern cousin.

Everybody today selling toys, all of them damaged with water and smelling of smoke. Because a big toy warehouse on Halsted Street burned down yesterday—see there?—the smoke still rising and drifting across the Dan Ryan expressway. And now there is a big fire sale at Maxwell Street, today only.

So what if we didn't get our new Bendable Legs Barbie and Midge and Ken and Skipper and Tutti and Todd and Scooter and Ricky and Alan and Francie in nice clean boxes and had to buy them on Maxwell Street, all water-soaked and sooty. So what if our Barbies smell like smoke when you hold them up to your nose even after you wash and wash and wash them. And if the prettiest doll, Barbie's MOD'ern cousin Francie with real eyelashes, eyelash brush included, has a left foot that's melted a little—so? If you dress her in her new "Prom Pinks" outfit, satin splendor with matching coat, gold belt, clutch, and hair bow included, so long as you don't lift her dress, right?—who's to know.

Fool's Paradise

Isaac Bashevis Singer

Somewhere, sometime, there lived a rich man whose name was Kadish. He had an only son who was called Atzel. In the household of Kadish there lived a distant relative, an orphan girl, called Aksah. Atzel was a tall boy with black hair and black eyes. Aksah was somewhat shorter than Atzel, and she had blue eyes and golden hair. Both were about the same age. As children, they ate together, studied together, played together. Atzel played the husband; Aksah, his wife. It was taken for granted that when they grew up they would really marry.

But when they had grown up, Atzel suddenly became ill. It was a sickness no one had ever heard of before: Atzel imagined that he was dead.

How did such an idea come to him? It seems it came from listening to stories about paradise. He had had an old nurse who had constantly described the place to him. She had told him that in paradise it was not necessary to work or to study or make any effort whatsoever. In paradise one ate the meat of wild oxen and the flesh of whales; one drank the wine that the Lord reserved for the just; one slept late into the day; and one had no duties.

Atzel was lazy by nature. He hated to get up early in the morning and to study languages and science. He knew that one day he would have to take over his father's business and he did not want to.

Since his old nurse had told Atzel that the only way to get to paradise was to die, he had made up his mind to do just that as quickly as possible. He thought and brooded about it so much that soon he began to imagine that he *was* dead.

Of course his parents became terribly worried when they saw what was happening to Atzel. Aksah cried in secret. The family did everything possible to try to convince Atzel that he was alive, but he refused to believe them. He would say, "Why don't you bury me? You see that I am dead. Because of you I cannot get to paradise."

Many doctors were called in to examine Atzel, and all tried to convince the boy that he was alive. They pointed out that he was talking, eating, and sleeping. But before long Atzel began to eat less and he rarely spoke. His family feared that he would die.

In despair, Kadish went to consult a great specialist, celebrated for his knowledge and wisdom. His name was Dr. Yoetz. After listening to a description of Atzel's illness, he said to Kadish, "I promise to cure your son in eight days, on one condition. You must do whatever I tell you to, no matter how strange it may seem."

Kadish agreed, and Dr. Yoetz said he would visit Atzel that same day. Kadish went home to prepare the household. He told his wife, Aksah, and the servants that all were to follow the doctor's orders without question, and they did so.

When Dr. Yoetz arrived, he was taken to Atzel's room. The boy lay on his bed, pale and thin from fasting, his hair disheveled, his nightclothes wrinkled.

The doctor took one look at Atzel and called out, "Why do you keep a dead body in the house? Why don't you make a funeral?"

On hearing these words the parents became terribly frightened, but Atzel's face lit up with a smile and he said, "You see, I was right."

Although Kadish and his wife were bewildered by the doctor's words, they remembered Kadish's promise, and went immediately to make arrangements for the funeral.

Atzel now became so excited by what the doctor had said that he jumped out of bed and began to dance and clap his hands. His joy made him hungry and he asked for food. But Dr. Yoetz replied, "Wait, you will eat in paradise."

The doctor requested that a room be prepared to look like paradise. The walls were hung with white satin, and precious rugs covered the floors. The windows were shuttered, and draperies tightly drawn. Candles and oil lamps burned day and night. The servants were dressed in white with wings on their backs and were to play angels.

Atzel was placed in an open coffin, and a funeral ceremony was held. Atzel was so exhausted with happiness that he slept right through it. When he awoke, he found himself in a room he didn't recognize. "Where am I?" he asked.

"In paradise, my lord," a winged servant replied.

"I'm terribly hungry," Atzel said. "I'd like some whale flesh and sacred wine."

"In a moment, my lord."

The chief servant clapped his hands and a door opened through which there came men servants and maids, all with wings on their backs, bearing golden trays laden with meat, fish, pomegranates and persimmons, pineapples and peaches. A tall servant with a long white beard carried a golden goblet full of wine. Atzel was so starved that he ate ravenously. The angels hovered around him, filling his plate and goblet even before he had time to ask for more.

When he had finished eating, Atzel declared he wanted to rest. Two angels undressed and bathed him. Then they brought him a nightdress of fine embroidered linen, placed a nightcap with a tassel on his head, and carried him to a bed with silken sheets and a purple velvet canopy. Atzel immediately fell into a deep and happy sleep.

When he awoke, it was morning but it could just as well have been night. The shutters were closed, and the candles and oil lamps were burning. As soon as the servants saw that Atzel was awake, they brought in exactly the same meal as the day before.

"Why do you give me the same food as yesterday?" Atzel asked. "Don't you have any milk, coffee, fresh rolls, and butter?"

"No, my lord. In paradise one always eats the same food," the servant replied.

"Is it already day, or is it still night?" Atzel asked.

"In paradise there is neither day nor night."

Dr. Yoetz had given careful instructions on how the servants were to talk to Atzel and behave toward him.

Atzel again ate the fish, meat, fruit, and drank the wine, but his appetite was not as good as it had been. When he had finished his meal and washed his hands in a golden finger bowl, he asked, "What time is it?"

"In paradise time does not exist," the servant answered.

"What shall I do now?" Atzel questioned.

"In paradise, my lord, one doesn't do anything."

"Where are the other saints?" Atzel inquired. "I'd like to meet them."

"In paradise each family has a place of its own."

"Can't one go visiting?"

"In paradise the dwellings are too far from each other for visiting. It would take thousands of years to go from one to the other."

"When will my family come?" Atzel asked.

"Your father still has twenty years to live, your mother thirty. And as long as they live they can't come here."

"What about Aksah?"

"She has more than fifty years to live."

"Do I have to be alone all that time?"

"Yes, my lord."

For a while Atzel shook his head, pondering. Then he asked, "What is Aksah going to do?"

"Right now, she's mourning for you. But you know, my lord, that one cannot mourn forever. Sooner or later she will forget you, meet another young man, and marry. That's how it is with the living."

Atzel got up and began to walk to and fro. His long sleep and the rich food had restored his energy. For the first time in years lazy Atzel had a desire to do something, but there was nothing to do in his paradise.

For eight days Atzel remained in his false heaven, and from day to day he became sadder and sadder. He missed his father; he longed for his mother; he yearned for Aksah. Idleness did not appeal to him as it had in former times. Now he wished he had something to study; he dreamed of traveling; he wanted to ride his horse, to talk to friends. The food, which had so delighted him the first day, lost its flavor.

The time came when he could no longer conceal his sadness. He remarked to one of the servants, "I see now that it is not as bad to live as I had thought."

"To live, my lord, is difficult. One has to study, work, do business. Here everything is easy," the servant consoled him.

"I would rather chop wood and carry stones than sit here. And how long will this last?"

"Forever."

"Stay here forever?" Atzel began to tear his hair in grief. "I'd rather kill myself."

"A dead man cannot kill himself."

On the eighth day, when it seemed that Atzel had reached the deepest despair, one of the servants, as had been arranged, came to him and said, "My lord, there has been a mistake. You are not dead. You must leave paradise."

"I'm alive?"

"Yes, you are alive, and I will bring you back to earth."

Atzel was beside himself with joy. The servant blindfolded him, and after leading him back and forth through the long corridors of the house, brought him to the room where his family was waiting and uncovered his eyes.

It was a bright day, and the sun shone through the open windows. A breeze from the surrounding fields and orchards freshened the air. In the garden outside, the birds were singing and the bees buzzing as they flew from flower to flower. From the barns and stables Atzel could hear the mooing of cows and the neighing of horses. Joyfully he embraced and kissed his parents and Aksah.

"I didn't know how good it was to be alive," he cried out.

And to Aksah he said: "Haven't you met another young man while I was away? Do you still love me?"

"Yes, I do, Atzel. I could not forget you."

"If that is so, it is time we got married."

It was not long before the wedding took place. Dr. Yoetz was the guest of honor. Musicians played; guests came from faraway cities. Some came on horseback, some drove mules, and some rode camels. All brought fine gifts for the bride and groom, in gold, silver, ivory, and assorted precious stones. The celebration lasted seven days and seven nights. It was one of the gayest weddings that old men had ever remembered. Atzel and Aksah were extremely happy, and both lived to a ripe old age. Atzel stopped being lazy and became the most diligent merchant in the whole region. His trading caravans traveled as far as Baghdad and India.

It was not until after the wedding that Atzel learned how Dr. Yoetz had cured him, and that he had lived in a fool's paradise. In the years to come he often talked with Aksah about his adventures, and later they told the tale of Dr. Yoetz's wonderful cure to their children and grandchildren, always finishing with the words, "But, of course, what paradise is really like, no one can tell."

The Censors

Luisa Valenzuela

Poor Juan! One day they caught him with his guard down before he could even realize that what he had taken as a stroke of luck was really one of fate's dirty tricks. These things happen the minute you're careless and you let down your guard, as one often does. Juancito let happiness—a feeling you can't trust—get the better of him when he received from a confidential source Mariana's new address in Paris and he knew that she hadn't forgotten him. Without thinking twice, he sat down at his table and wrote her a letter. *The* letter that keeps his mind off his job during the day and won't let him sleep at night (what had he scrawled, what had he put on that sheet of paper he sent to Mariana?).

Juan knows there won't be a problem with the letter's contents, that it's irreproachable, harmless. But what about the rest? He knows that they examine, sniff, feel, and read between the lines of each and every letter, and check its tiniest comma and most accidental stain. He knows that all letters pass from hand to hand and go through all sorts of tests in the huge censorship offices and that, in the end, very few continue on their way. Usually it takes months, even years, if there aren't any snags; all this time the freedom, maybe even the life, of both sender and receiver is in jeopardy. And that's why Juan's so down in the dumps: thinking that something might happen to Mariana because of his letters. Of all people, Mariana, who must finally feel safe there where she always dreamed she'd live. But he knows that the *Censor's Secret Command* operates all over the world and cashes in on the discount in air rates; there's nothing to stop them from going as far as that hidden Paris neighborhood, kidnapping Mariana, and returning to their cozy homes, certain of having fulfilled their noble mission.

Well, you've got to beat them to the punch, do what everyone tries to do: sabotage the machinery, throw sand in its gears, get to the bottom of the problem so as to stop it.

This was Juan's sound plan when he, like many others, applied for a censor's job—not because he had a calling or needed a job: no, he applied simply to intercept his own letter, a consoling but unoriginal idea. He was hired immediately, for each day more and more censors are needed and no one would bother to check on his references.

Ulterior motives couldn't be overlooked by the *Censorship Division,* but they needn't be too strict with those who applied. They knew how hard it would be for those poor guys to find the letter they wanted and even if they did, what's a letter or two when the new censor would snap up so many others? That's how Juan managed to join the *Post Office's Censorship Division,* with a certain goal in mind.

The building had a festive air on the outside which contrasted with its inner staidness. Little by little, Juan was absorbed by his job and he felt at peace since he was doing everything he could to get his letter for Mariana. He didn't even worry when, in his first month, he was sent to *Section K* where envelopes are very carefully screened for explosives.

It's true that on the third day, a fellow worker had his right hand blown off by a letter, but the division chief claimed it was sheer negligence on the victim's part. Juan and the other employees were allowed to go back to their work, albeit feeling less secure. After work, one of them tried to organize a strike to demand higher wages for unhealthy work, but Juan didn't join in; after thinking it over, he reported him to his superiors and thus got promoted.

You don't form a habit by doing something once, he told himself as he left his boss's office. And when he was transferred to *Section J,* where letters are carefully checked for poison dust, he felt he had climbed a rung in the ladder.

By working hard, he quickly reached *Section E* where the work was more interesting, for he could now read and analyze the letters' contents. Here he could even hope to get hold of his letter which, judging by the time that had elapsed, had gone through the other sections and was probably floating around in this one.

Soon his work became so absorbing that his noble mission blurred in his mind. Day after day he crossed out whole paragraphs in red ink, pitilessly chucking many letters into the censored basket. These were horrible days when he was shocked by the subtle and conniving ways employed by people to pass on subversive messages; his instincts were so sharp that he found behind a simple "the weather's unsettled" or "prices continue to soar" the wavering hand of someone secretly scheming to overthrow the Government.

His zeal brought him swift promotion. We don't know if this made him happy. Very few letters reached him in *Section B*—only a handful passed the other hurdles—so he read them over and over again, passed them under a magnifying glass, searched for microprint with an electronic microscope, and tuned his sense of smell so that he was beat by the time he made it home. He'd barely manage to warm up his soup, eat some fruit, and fall into bed, satisfied with having done his duty. Only his darling mother worried, but she couldn't get him back on the right road. She'd say, though it wasn't always true: Lola called, she's at the bar with the girls, they miss you, they're waiting for you. Or else she'd leave a bottle of red wine on the table. But Juan wouldn't overdo it: any distraction could make him lose his edge and the perfect censor had to be alert, keen, attentive, and sharp to nab cheats. He had a truly patriotic task, both self-denying and uplifting.

His basket for censored letters became the best fed as well as the most cunning basket in the whole *Censorship Division.* He was about to congratulate himself for having finally discovered his true mission, when his letter to Mariana reached his hands. Naturally, he censored it without regret. And just as naturally, he couldn't stop them from executing him the following morning, another victim of his devotion to his work.

The Man that Corrupted Hadleyburg

Mark Twain

It was many years ago. Hadleyburg was the most honest and upright town in all the region a round about. It had kept that reputation unsmirched during three generations, and was prouder of it than of any other of its possessions. It was so proud of it, and so anxious to insure its perpetuation, that it began to teach the principles of honest dealing to its babies in the cradle, and made the like teachings the staple of their culture thenceforward through all the years devoted to their education. Also, throughout the formative years temptations were kept out of the way of the young people, so that their honesty could have every chance to harden and solidify, and become a part of their very bone. The neighbouring towns were jealous of this honorable supremacy, and affected to sneer at Hadleyburg's pride in it and call it vanity; but all the same they were obliged to acknowledge that Hadleyburg was in reality an incorruptible town; and if pressed they would also acknowledge that the mere fact that a young man hailed from Hadleyburg was all the recommendation he needed when he went forth from his natal town to seek for responsible employment.

But at last, in the drift of time, Hadleyburg had the ill luck to offend a passing stranger—possibly without knowing it, certainly without caring, for Hadleyburg was sufficient unto itself, and cared not a rap for strangers or their opinions. Still, it would have been well to make an exception in this one's case, for he was a bitter man and revengeful. All through his wanderings during a whole year he kept his injury in mind, and gave all his leisure moments to trying to invent a compensating satisfaction for it. He contrived many plans, and all of them were good, but none of them was quite sweeping enough: the poorest of them would hurt a great many individuals, but what he wanted was a plan which would comprehend the entire town, and not let so much as one person escape unhurt. At last he had a fortunate idea, and when it fell into his brain it lit up his whole head with an evil joy. He began to form a plan at once, saying to himself "That is the thing to do—I will corrupt the town."

Six months later he went to Hadleyburg, and arrived in a buggy at the house of the old cashier of the bank about ten at night. He got a sack out of the buggy, shouldered it, and staggered with it through the cottage yard, and knocked at the door. A woman's voice said "Come in," and he entered, and set his sack behind the stove in the parlor, saying politely to the old lady who sat reading the *Missionary Herald* by the lamp:

"Pray keep your seat, madam, I will not disturb you. There—now it is pretty well concealed; one would hardly know it was there. Can I see your husband a moment, madam?"

No, he was gone to Brixton, and might not return before morning.

"Very well, madam, it is no matter. I merely wanted to leave that sack in his care, to be delivered to the rightful owner when he shall be found. I am a stranger; he does not know me; I am merely passing through the town to-night to discharge a matter which has been long in my mind. My errand is now completed, and I go pleased and a little proud, and you will never see me again. There is a paper attached to the sack which will explain everything. Good-night, madam."

The old lady was afraid of the mysterious big stranger, and was glad to see him go. But her curiosity was roused, and she went straight to the sack and brought away the paper. It began as follows:

TO BE PUBLISHED,

or, the right man sought out by private inquiry—either will answer. This sack contains gold coin weighing a hundred and sixty pounds four ounces—"

"Mercy on us, and the door not locked!"

Mrs. Richards flew to it all in a tremble and locked it, then pulled down the window-shades and stood frightened, worried, and wondering if there was anything else she could do toward making herself and the money more safe. She listened awhile for burglars, then surrendered to curiosity, and went back to the lamp and finished reading the paper:

I am a foreigner, and am presently going back to my own country, to remain there permanently. I am grateful to America for what I have received at her hands during my long stay under her flag; and to one of her citizens—a citizen of Hadleyburg—I am especially grateful for a great kindness, done me a year or two ago. Two great kindnesses, in fact. I will explain. I was a gambler. I say I WAS. I was a ruined gambler. I arrived in this village at night, hungry and without a penny. I asked for help—in the dark; I was ashamed to beg in the light. I begged of the right man. He gave me twenty dollars—that is to say, he gave me life, as I considered it. He also gave me fortune; for out of that money I have made myself rich at the gaming-table. And finally, a remark which he made to me has remained with me to this day, and has at last conquered me; and in conquering has saved the remnant of my morals; I shall gamble no more. Now I have no idea who that man was, but I want him found, and I want him to have this money, to give away, throw away, or keep, as he pleases. It is merely my way of testifying my gratitude to him. If I could stay, I would find him myself; but no matter, he will be found. This is an honest town, an incorruptible town, and I know I can trust it without fear. This man can be identified by the remark which he made to me; I feel persuaded that he will remember it.

And now my plan is this: If you prefer to conduct the inquiry privately, do so. Tell the contents of this present writing to any one who is likely to be the right man. If he shall answer, 'I am the man; the remark I made was so-and-so,' apply the test—to wit: open the sack, and in it you will find a sealed envelope containing that remark. If the remark mentioned by the candidate tallies with it, give him the money, and ask no further questions, for he is certainly the right man.

But if you shall prefer a public inquiry, then publish this present writing in the local paper—with these instructions added, to wit: Thirty days from now, let the candidate appear at the town-hall at eight in the evening (Friday), and hand his remark, in a sealed envelope, to the Rev. Mr. Burgess (if he will be kind enough to act); and let Mr. Burgess there and then destroy the seals of the sack, open it, and see if the remark is correct: if correct, let the money be delivered, with my sincere gratitude, to my benefactor thus identified.

Mrs. Richards sat down, gently quivering with excitement, and was soon lost in thinkings—after this pattern: "What a strange thing it is! . . . And what a fortune for that kind man who set his bread afloat upon the waters! . . . If it had only been my husband that did it!—for we are so poor, so old and poor! . . ." Then, with a sigh—"But it was not my Edward; no, it was not he that gave a stranger twenty dollars. It is a pity too; I see it now . . ." Then, with a shudder—"But it is *gambler's* money! the wages of sin: we couldn't take it; we couldn't touch it. I don't like to be near it; it seems a defilement." She moved to a farther chair. . . . "I wish Edward would come and take it to the bank; a burglar might come at any moment; it is dreadful to be here all alone with it."

At eleven Mr. Richards arrived, and while his wife was saying "I am *so* glad you've come!" he was saying, "I'm so tired—tired clear out; it is dreadful to be poor, and have to make these dismal journeys at my time of life. Always at the grind, grind, grind, on a salary—another man's slave, and he sitting at home in his slippers, rich and comfortable."

"I am so sorry for you, Edward, you know that; but be comforted; we have our livelihood; we have our good name—"

"Yes, Mary, and that is everything. Don't mind my talk—it's just a moment's irritation and doesn't mean anything. Kiss me—there, it's all gone now, and I am not complaining any more. What have you been getting? What's in the sack?"

Then his wife told him the great secret. It dazed him for a moment; then he said:

"It weighs a hundred and sixty pounds? Why, Mary, it's forty thousand dollars—think of it—a whole fortune! Not ten men in this village are worth that much. Give me the paper."

He skimmed through it and said:

"Isn't it an adventure! Why, it's a romance; it's like the impossible things one reads about in books, and never sees in life." He was well stirred up now; cheerful, even gleeful. He tapped his old wife on the cheek, and said, humorously, "Why, we're rich, Mary, rich; all we've got to do is to bury the money and burn the papers. If the gambler ever comes to inquire, we'll merely look coldly upon him and say: 'What is this nonsense you are talking? We have never heard of you and your sack of gold before;' and then he would look foolish, and—"

"And in the meantime, while you are running on with your jokes, the money is still here, and it is fast getting along toward burglar- time."

"True. Very well, what shall we do—make the inquiry private? No, not that; it would spoil the romance. The public method is better. Think what a noise it will make! And it will make all the other towns jealous; for no stranger would trust such a thing to any town but Hadleyburg, and they know it. It's a great card for us. I must get to the printing-office now, or I shall be too late."

"But stop—stop—don't leave me here alone with it, Edward!"

But he was gone. For only a little while, however. Not far from his own house he met the editor-proprietor of the paper, and gave him the document, and said, "Here is a good thing for you, Cox—put it in."

"It may be too late, Mr. Richards, but I'll see."

At home again, he and his wife sat down to talk the charming mystery over; they were in no condition for sleep. The first question was, Who could the citizen have been who gave the stranger the twenty dollars? It seemed a simple one; both answered it in the same breath—

"Barclay Goodson."

"Yes," said Richards, "he could have done it, and it would have been like him, but there's not another in the town."

"Everybody will grant that, Edward—grant it privately, anyway. For six months, now, the village has been its own proper self once more—honest, narrow, self-righteous, and stingy."

"It is what he always called it, to the day of his death—said it right out publicly, too."

"Yes, and he was hated for it."

"Oh, of course; but he didn't care. I reckon he was the best-hated man among us, except the Reverend Burgess."

"Well, Burgess deserves it—he will never get another congregation here. Mean as the town is, it knows how to estimate *him*. Edward, doesn't it seem odd that the stranger should appoint Burgess to deliver the money?"

"Well, yes—it does. That is—that is—"

"Why so much that-*is*-ing? Would *you* select him?"

"Mary, maybe the stranger knows him better than this village does."

"Much *that* would help Burgess!"

The husband seemed perplexed for an answer; the wife kept a steady eye upon him, and waited. Finally Richards said, with the hesitancy of one who is making a statement which is likely to encounter doubt, "Mary, Burgess is not a bad man."

His wife was certainly surprised.

"Nonsense!" she exclaimed.

"He is not a bad man. I know. The whole of his unpopularity had its foundation in that one thing—the thing that made so much noise."

"That 'one thing,' indeed! As if that 'one thing' wasn't enough, all by itself."

"Plenty. Plenty. Only he wasn't guilty of it."

"How you talk! Not guilty of it! Everybody knows he *was* guilty."

"Mary, I give you my word—he was innocent."

"I can't believe it and I don't. How do you know?"

"It is a confession. I am ashamed, but I will make it. I was the only man who knew he was innocent. I could have saved him, and—and—well, you know how the town was wrought up—I hadn't the pluck to do it. It would have turned everybody against me. I felt mean, ever so mean; but I didn't dare; I hadn't the manliness to face that."

Mary looked troubled, and for a while was silent. Then she said stammeringly:

"I—I don't think it would have done for you to—to—One mustn't—er—public opinion—one has to be so careful—so—" It was a difficult road, and she got mired; but after a little she got started again. "It was a great pity, but—Why, we couldn't afford it, Edward—we couldn't indeed. Oh, I wouldn't have had you do it for anything!"

"It would have lost us the goodwill of so many people, Mary; and then—and then—"

"What troubles me now is, what *he* thinks of us, Edward."

"He? *He* doesn't suspect that I could have saved him."

"Oh," exclaimed the wife, in a tone of relief, "I am glad of that. As long as he doesn't know that you could have saved him, he—he—well, that makes it a great deal better. Why, I might have known he didn't know, because he is always trying to be friendly with us, as little encouragement as we give him. More than once people have twitted me with it. There's the Wilsons, and the Wilcoxes, and the Harknesses, they take a mean pleasure in saying *'your friend* Burgess,' because they know it pesters me. I wish he wouldn't persist in liking us so; I can't think why he keeps it up."

"I can explain it. It's another confession. When the thing was new and hot, and the town made a plan to ride him on a rail, my conscience hurt me so that I couldn't stand it, and I went privately and gave him notice, and he got out of the town and stayed out till it was safe to come back."

"Edward! If the town had found it out—"

"Don't! It scares me yet, to think of it. I repented of it the minute it was done; and I was even afraid to tell you lest your face might betray it to somebody. I didn't sleep any that night, for worrying. But after a few days I saw that no one was going to suspect me, and after that I got to feeling glad I did it. And I feel glad yet, Mary—glad through and through."

"So do I, now, for it would have been a dreadful way to treat him. Yes, I'm glad; for really you did owe him that, you know. But, Edward, suppose it should come out yet, some day!"

"It won't."

"Why?"

"Because everybody thinks it was Goodson."

"Of course they would!"

"Certainly. And of course *he* didn't care. They persuaded poor old Sawlsberry to go and charge it on him, and he went blustering over there and did it. Goodson looked him over, like as if he was hunting for a place on him that he could despise the most; then he says, 'So you are the Committee of Inquiry, are you?' Sawlsberry said that was about what he was. 'H'm. Do they require particulars, or do you reckon a kind of a *general* answer will do?' 'If they require particulars, I will come back, Mr. Goodson; I will take the general answer first.' 'Very well, then, tell them to go to hell—I reckon that's general enough. And I'll give you some advice, Sawlsberry; when you come back for the particulars, fetch a basket to carry the relics of yourself home in.'"

"Just like Goodson; it's got all the marks. He had only one vanity; he thought he could give advice better than any other person."

"It settled the business, and saved us, Mary. The subject was dropped."

"Bless you, I'm not doubting *that.*"

Then they took up the gold-sack mystery again, with strong interest. Soon the conversation began to suffer breaks—interruptions caused by absorbed thinkings. The breaks grew more and more frequent. At last Richards lost himself wholly in thought. He sat long, gazing vacantly at the floor, and by-and-by he began to punctuate his thoughts with little nervous movements of his hands that seemed to indicate vexation. Meantime his wife too had relapsed into a thoughtful silence, and her movements were beginning to show a troubled discomfort. Finally Richards got up and strode aimlessly about the room, ploughing his hands through his hair, much as a somnambulist might do who was having a bad dream. Then he seemed to arrive at a definite purpose; and without a word he put on his hat and passed quickly out of the house. His wife sat brooding, with a drawn face, and did not seem to be aware that she was alone. Now and then she murmured, "Lead us not into t . . . but—but—we are so poor, so poor! . . . Lead us not into . . . Ah, who would be hurt by it?—and no one would ever know . . . Lead us . . ." The voice died out in mumblings. After a little she glanced up and muttered in a half-frightened, half-glad way:

"He is gone! But, oh dear, he may be too late—too late . . . Maybe not—maybe there is still time." She rose and stood thinking, nervously clasping and unclasping her hands. A slight shudder shook her frame, and she said, out of a dry throat, "God forgive me—it's awful to think such things—but . . . Lord, how we are made—how strangely we are made!"

She turned the light low, and slipped stealthily over and knelt down by the sack and felt of its ridgy sides with her hands, and fondled them lovingly; and there was a gloating light in her poor old eyes. She fell into fits of absence; and came half out of them at times to mutter "If we had only waited!—oh, if we had only waited a little, and not been in such a hurry!"

Meantime Cox had gone home from his office and told his wife all about the strange thing that had happened, and they had talked it over eagerly, and guessed that the late Goodson was the only man in the town who could have helped a suffering stranger with so noble a sum as twenty dollars. Then there was a pause, and the two became thoughtful and silent. And by-and-by nervous and fidgety. At last the wife said, as if to herself,

"Nobody knows this secret but the Richardses . . . and us . . . nobody."

The husband came out of his thinkings with a slight start, and gazed wistfully at his wife, whose face was become very pale; then he hesitatingly rose, and glanced furtively at his hat, then at his wife—a sort of mute inquiry. Mrs. Cox swallowed once or twice, with her hand at her throat, then in place of speech she nodded her head. In a moment she was alone, and mumbling to herself.

And now Richards and Cox were hurrying through the deserted streets, from opposite directions. They met, panting, at the foot of the printing-office stairs; by the night-light there they read each other's face. Cox whispered:

"Nobody knows about this but us?"

The whispered answer was,

"Not a soul—on honor, not a soul!"

"If it isn't too late to—"

The men were starting up-stairs; at this moment they were overtaken by a boy, and Cox asked,

"Is that you, Johnny?"

"Yes, sir."

"You needn't ship the early mail—nor *any* mail; wait till I tell you."

"It's already gone, sir."

"Gone?" It had the sound of an unspeakable disappointment in it.

"Yes, sir. Time-table for Brixton and all the towns beyond changed to-day, sir—had to get the papers in twenty minutes earlier than common. I had to rush; if I had been two minutes later—"

The men turned and walked slowly away, not waiting to hear the rest. Neither of them spoke during ten minutes; then Cox said, in a vexed tone,

"What possessed you to be in such a hurry, I can't make out."

The answer was humble enough:

"I see it now, but somehow I never thought, you know, until it was too late. But the next time—"

"Next time be hanged! It won't come in a thousand years."

Then the friends separated without a good-night, and dragged themselves home with the gait of mortally stricken men. At their homes their wives sprang up with an eager "Well?"—then saw the answer with their eyes and sank down sorrowing, without waiting for it to come in words. In both houses a discussion followed of a heated sort—a new thing; there had been discussions before, but not heated ones, not ungentle ones. The discussions to-night were a sort of seeming plagiarisms of each other. Mrs. Richards said:

"If you had only waited, Edward—if you had only stopped to think; but no, you must run straight to the printing-office and spread it all over the world."

"It *said* publish it."

"That is nothing; it also said do it privately, if you liked. There, now—is that true, or not?"

"Why, yes—yes, it is true; but when I thought what a stir it would make, and what a compliment it was to Hadleyburg that a stranger should trust it so—"

"Oh, certainly, I know all that; but if you had only stopped to think, you would have seen that you *couldn't* find the right man, because he is in his grave, and hasn't left chick nor child nor relation behind him; and as long as the money went to somebody that awfully needed it, and nobody would be hurt by it, and—and—"

She broke down, crying. Her husband tried to think of some comforting thing to say, and presently came out with this:

"But after all, Mary, it must be for the best—it *must* be; we know that. And we must remember that it was so ordered—"

"Ordered! Oh, everything's *ordered,* when a person has to find some way out when he has been stupid. Just the same, it was *ordered* that the money should come to us in this special way, and it was you that must take it on yourself to go meddling with the designs of Providence—and who gave you the right? It was wicked, that is what it was—just blasphemous presumption, and no more becoming to a meek and humble professor of—"

"But, Mary, you know how we have been trained all our lives long, like the whole village, till it is absolutely second nature to us to stop not a single moment to think when there's an honest thing to be done—"

"Oh, I know it, I know it—it's been one everlasting training and training and training in honesty—honesty shielded, from the very cradle, against every possible temptation, and so it's *artificial* honesty, and weak as water when temptation comes, as we have seen this night. God knows I never had shade nor shadow of a doubt of my petrified and indestructible honesty until now—and now, under the very first big and real temptation, I—Edward, it is my belief that this town's honesty is as rotten as mine is; as rotten as yours is. It is a mean town, a hard, stingy town, and hasn't a virtue in the world but this honesty it is so celebrated for and so conceited about; and so help me, I do believe that if ever the day comes that its honesty falls under great temptation, its grand reputation will go to ruin like a house of cards. There, now, I've made confession, and I feel better; I am a humbug, and I've been one all my life, without knowing it. Let no man call me honest again—I will not have it."

"I—Well, Mary, I feel a good deal as you do: I certainly do. It seems strange, too, so strange. I never could have believed it—never."

A long silence followed; both were sunk in thought. At last the wife looked up and said:

"I know what you are thinking, Edward."

Richards had the embarrassed look of a person who is caught.

"I am ashamed to confess it, Mary, but—"

"It's no matter, Edward, I was thinking the same question myself."

"I hope so. State it."

"You were thinking, if a body could only guess out *what the remark was* that Goodson made to the stranger."

"It's perfectly true. I feel guilty and ashamed. And you?"

"I'm past it. Let us make a pallet here; we've got to stand watch till the bank vault opens in the morning and admits the sack. . . Oh dear, oh dear—if we hadn't made the mistake!"

The pallet was made, and Mary said:

"The open sesame—what could it have been? I do wonder what that remark could have been. But come; we will get to bed now."

"And sleep?"

"No; think."

"Yes; think."

By this time the Coxes too had completed their spat and their reconciliation, and were turning in—to think, to think, and toss, and fret, and worry over what the remark could possibly have been which Goodson made to the stranded derelict; that golden remark; that remark worth forty thousand dollars, cash.

The reason that the village telegraph-office was open later than usual that night was this: The foreman of Cox's paper was the local representative of the Associated Press. One might say its honorary representative, for it wasn't four times a year that he could furnish thirty words that would be accepted. But this time it was different. His despatch stating what he had caught got an instant answer:

"Send the whole thing—all the details—twelve hundred words."

A colossal order! The foreman filled the bill; and he was the proudest man in the State. By breakfast-time the next morning the name of Hadleyburg the Incorruptible was on every lip in America, from Montreal to the Gulf, from the glaciers of Alaska to the orange-groves of Florida; and millions and millions of people were discussing the stranger and his money-sack, and wondering if the right man would be found, and hoping some more news about the matter would come soon—right away.

II

Hadleyburg village woke up world-celebrated—astonished—happy—vain. Vain beyond imagination. Its nineteen principal citizens and their wives went about shaking hands with each other, and beaming, and smiling, and congratulating, and saying *this* thing adds a new word to the dictionary—*Hadleyburg,* synonym for *incorruptible*—desined to live in dictionaries for ever! And the minor and unimportant citizens and their wives went around acting in much the same way. Everybody ran to the bank to see the gold-sack; and before noon grieved and envious crowds began to flock in from Brixton and all neighbouring towns; and that afternoon and next day reporters began to arrive from everywhere to verify the sack and its history and write the whole thing up anew, and make dashing free-hand pictures of the sack, and of Richards's house, and the bank, and the Presbyterian church, and the Baptist church, and the public square, and the town-hall where the test would be applied and the money delivered; and damnable portraits of the Richardses, and Pinkerton the banker, and Cox, and the foreman, and Reverend Burgess, and the postmaster—and even of Jack Halliday, who was the loafing, good-natured, no-account, irreverent fisherman, hunter, boys' friend, stray-dogs' friend, typical "Sam Lawson" of the town. The little mean, smirking, oily Pinkerton showed the sack to all comers, and rubbed his sleek palms together pleasantly, and enlarged upon the town's fine old reputation for honesty and upon this wonderful endorsement of it, and hoped and believed that the example would now spread far and wide over the American world, and be epoch-making in the matter of moral regeneration. And so on, and so on.

By the end of a week things had quieted down again; the wild intoxication of pride and joy had sobered to a soft, sweet, silent delight—a sort of deep, nameless, unutterable content. All faces bore a look of peaceful, holy happiness.

Then a change came. It was a gradual change; so gradual that its beginnings were hardly noticed; maybe were not noticed at all, except by Jack Halliday, who always noticed everything; and always made fun of it, too, no matter what it was. He began to throw out chaffing remarks about people not looking quite so happy as they did a day or two ago; and next he claimed that the new aspect was deepening to positive sadness; next, that it was taking on a sick look; and finally he said that everybody was become so moody, thoughtful, and absent-minded that he could rob the meanest man in town of a cent out of the bottom of his breeches pocket and not disturb his reverie.

At this stage—or at about this stage—a saying like this was dropped at bedtime—with a sigh, usually—by the head of each of the nineteen principal households:

"Ah, what *could* have been the remark that Goodson made?"

And straightway—with a shudder—came this, from the man's wife:

"Oh, *don't*! What horrible thing are you mulling in your mind? Put it away from you, for God's sake!"

But that question was wrung from those men again the next night—and got the same retort. But weaker.

And the third night the men uttered the question yet again—with anguish, and absently. This time—and the following night—the wives fidgeted feebly, and tried to say something. But didn't.

And the night after that they found their tongues and responded—longingly:

"Oh, if we *could* only guess!"

Halliday's comments grew daily more and more sparklingly disagreeable and disparaging. He went diligently about, laughing at the town, individually and in mass. But his laugh was the only one left in the village: it fell upon a hollow and mournful vacancy and emptiness. Not even a smile was findable anywhere. Halliday carried a cigar-box around on a tripod, playing that it was a camera, and halted all passers and aimed the thing and said "Ready!—now look pleasant, please," but not even this capital joke could surprise the dreary faces into any softening.

So three weeks passed—one week was left. It was Saturday evening after supper. Instead of the aforetime Saturday-evening flutter and bustle and shopping and larking, the streets were empty and desolate. Richards and his old wife sat apart in their little parlour—miserable and thinking. This was become their evening habit now: the life-long habit which had preceded it, of reading, knitting, and contented chat, or receiving or paying neighborly calls, was dead and gone and forgotten, ages ago—two or three weeks ago; nobody talked now, nobody read, nobody visited—the whole village sat at home, sighing, worrying, silent. Trying to guess out that remark.

The postman left a letter. Richards glanced listlessly at the superscription and the post-mark—unfamiliar, both—and tossed the letter on the table and resumed his might-have-beens and his hopeless dull miseries where he had left them off. Two or three hours later his wife got wearily up and was going away to bed without a good-night—custom now—but she stopped near the letter and eyed it awhile with a dead interest, then broke it open, and began to skim it over. Richards, sitting there with his chair tilted back against the wall and his chin between his knees, heard something fall. It was his wife. He sprang to her side, but she cried out:

"Leave me alone, I am too happy. Read the letter—read it!"

He did. He devoured it, his brain reeling. The letter was from a distant State, and it said:

I am a stranger to you, but no matter: I have something to tell. I have just arrived home from Mexico, and learned about that episode. Of course you do not know who made that remark, but I know, and I am the only person living who does know. It was GOODSON. I knew him well, many years ago. I passed through your village that very night, and was his guest till the midnight train came along. I overheard him make that remark to the stranger in the dark—it was in Hale Alley. He and I talked of it the rest of the way home, and while smoking in his house. He mentioned many of your villagers in the course of his talk—most of them in a very uncomplimentary way, but two or three favorably: among these latter yourself. I say 'favorably'—nothing stronger. I remember his saying he did not actually LIKE any person in the town—not one; but that you—I THINK he said you—am almost sure—had done him a very great service once, possibly without knowing the full value of it, and he wished he had a fortune, he would leave it to you when he died, and a curse apiece for the rest of the citizens. Now, then, if it was you that did him that service, you are his legitimate heir, and entitled to the sack of gold. I know that I can trust to your honor and honesty, for in a citizen of Hadleyburg these virtues are an unfailing inheritance, and so I am going to reveal to you the remark, well satisfied that if you are not the right man you will seek and find the right one and see that poor Goodson's debt of gratitude for the service referred to is paid. This is the remark 'YOU ARE FAR FROM BEING A BAD MAN: GO, AND REFORM.'

HOWARD L. STEPHENSON.

"Oh, Edward, the money is ours, and I am so grateful, *oh,* so grateful,—kiss me, dear, it's for ever since we kissed—and we needed it so—the money—and now you are free of Pinkerton and his bank, and nobody's slave any more; it seems to me I could fly for joy."

It was a happy half-hour that the couple spent there on the settee caressing each other; it was the old days come again—days that had begun with their courtship and lasted without a break till the stranger brought the deadly money. By-and-by the wife said:

"Oh, Edward, how lucky it was you did him that grand service, poor Goodson! I never liked him, but I love him now. And it was fine and beautiful of you never to mention it or brag about it." Then, with a touch of reproach, "But you ought to have told *me,* Edward, you ought to have told your wife, you know."

"Well, I—er—well, Mary, you see—"

"Now stop hemming and hawing, and tell me about it, Edward. I always loved you, and now I'm proud of you. Everybody believes there was only one good generous soul in this village, and now it turns out that you—Edward, why don't you tell me?"

"Well—er—er—Why, Mary, I can't!"

"You *can't*? *Why* can't you?"

"You see, he—well, he—he made me promise I wouldn't."

The wife looked him over, and said, very slowly:

"Made—you—promise? Edward, what do you tell me that for?"

"Mary, do you think I would lie?"

She was troubled and silent for a moment, then she laid her hand within his and said:

"No . . . no. We have wandered far enough from our bearings—God spare us that! In all your life you have never uttered a lie. But now—now that the foundations of things seem to be crumbling from under us, we—we—" She lost her voice for a moment, then said, brokenly, "Lead us not into temptation. . . I think you made the promise, Edward. Let it rest so. Let us keep away from that ground. Now—that is all gone by; let us be happy again; it is no time for clouds."

Edward found it something of an effort to comply, for his mind kept wandering—trying to remember what the service was that he had done Goodson.

The couple lay awake the most of the night, Mary happy and busy, Edward busy, but not so happy. Mary was planning what she would do with the money. Edward was trying to recall that service. At first his conscience was sore on account of the lie he had told Mary—if it was a lie. After much reflection—suppose it *was* a lie? What then? Was it such a great matter? Aren't we always *acting* lies? Then why not tell them? Look at Mary—look what she had done. While he was hurrying off on his honest errand, what was she doing? Lamenting because the papers hadn't been destroyed and the money kept. Is theft better than lying?

That point lost its sting—the lie dropped into the background and left comfort behind it. The next point came to the front: *Had* he rendered that service? Well, here was Goodson's own evidence as reported in Stephenson's letter; there could be no better evidence than that—it was even *proof* that he had rendered it. Of course. So that point was settled . . . No, not quite. He recalled with a wince that this unknown Mr. Stephenson was just a trifle unsure as to whether the performer of it was Richards or some other—and, oh dear, he had put Richards on his honor! He must himself decide whither that money must go—and Mr. Stephenson was not doubting that if he was the wrong man he would go honorably and find the right one. Oh, it was odious to put a man in such a situation—ah, why couldn't

Stephenson have left out that doubt? What did he want to intrude that for?

Further reflection. How did it happen that *Richards's* name remained in Stephenson's mind as indicating the right man, and not some other man's name? That looked good. Yes, that looked very good. In fact it went on looking better and better, straight along—until by-and-by it grew into positive *proof.* And then Richards put the matter at once out of his mind, for he had a private instinct that a proof once established is better left so.

He was feeling reasonably comfortable now, but there was still one other detail that kept pushing itself on his notice: of course he had done that service—that was settled; but what *was* that service? He must recall it—he would not go to sleep till he had recalled it; it would make his peace of mind perfect. And so he thought and thought. He thought of a dozen things—possible services, even probable services—but none of them seemed adequate, none of them seemed large enough, none of them seemed worth the money—worth the fortune Goodson had wished he could leave in his will. And besides, he couldn't remember having done them, anyway. Now, then—now, then—what *kind* of a service would it be that would make a man so inordinately grateful? Ah—the saving of his soul! That must be it. Yes, he could remember, now, how he once set himself the task of converting Goodson, and labored at it as much as—he was going to say three months; but upon closer examination it shrunk to a month, then to a week, then to a day, then to nothing. Yes, he remembered now, and with unwelcome vividness, that Goodson had told him to go to thunder and mind his own business—*he* wasn't hankering to follow Hadleyburg to heaven!

So that solution was a failure—he hadn't saved Goodson's soul. Richards was discouraged. Then after a little came another idea: had he saved Goodson's property? No, that wouldn't do—he hadn't any. His life? That is it! Of course. Why, he might have thought of it before. This time he was on the right track, sure. His imagination-mill was hard at work in a minute, now.

Thereafter, during a stretch of two exhausting hours, he was busy saving Goodson's life. He saved it in all kinds of difficult and perilous ways. In every case he got it saved satisfactorily up to a certain point; then, just as he was beginning to get well persuaded that it had really happened, a troublesome detail would turn up which made the whole thing impossible. As in the matter of drowning, for instance. In that case he had swum out and tugged Goodson ashore in an unconscious state with a great crowd looking on and applauding, but when he had got it all thought out and was just beginning to remember all about it, a whole swarm of disqualifying details arrived on the ground: the town would have known of the circumstance, Mary would have known of it, it would glare like a limelight in his own memory instead of being an inconspicuous service which he had possibly rendered "without knowing its full value." And at this point he remembered that he couldn't swim anyway.

Ah—*there* was a point which he had been overlooking from the start: it had to be a service which he had rendered "possibly without knowing the full value of it." Why, really, that ought to be an easy hunt—much easier than those others. And sure enough, by-and-by he found it. Goodson, years and years ago, came near marrying a very sweet and pretty girl, named Nancy Hewitt, but in some way or other the match had been broken off; the girl died, Goodson remained a bachelor, and by-and-by became a soured one and a frank despiser of the human species. Soon after the girl's death the village found out, or thought it had found out, that she carried a spoonful of negro blood in her veins. Richards worked at these details a good while, and in the end he thought he remembered things concerning them which must have gotten mislaid in his memory through long neglect. He seemed to dimly remember that it was *he* that found out about the negro blood; that it was he that told the village; that the village told Goodson where they got it; that he thus saved Goodson from marrying the tainted girl; that he had done him this great service "without knowing the full value of it," in fact without knowing that he *was* doing it; but that Goodson knew the value of it, and what a narrow escape he had had, and so went to his grave grateful to his benefactor and wishing he had a fortune to leave him. It was all clear and simple, now, and the more he went over it the more luminous and certain it grew; and at last, when he nestled to sleep, satisfied and happy, he remembered the whole thing just as if it had been yesterday. In fact, he dimly remembered Goodson's *telling* him his gratitude once. Meantime Mary had spent six thousand dollars on a new house for herself and a pair of slippers for her pastor, and then had fallen peacefully to rest.

That same Saturday evening the postman had delivered a letter to each of the other principal citizens—nineteen letters in all. No two of the envelopes were alike, and no two of the superscriptions were in the same hand, but the letters inside were just like each other in every detail but one. They were exact copies of the letter received by Richards—handwriting and all—and were all signed by Stephenson, but in place of Richards's name each receiver's own name appeared.

All night long eighteen principal citizens did what their caste-brother Richards was doing at the same time—they put in their energies trying to remember what notable service it was that they had unconsciously done Barclay Goodson. In no case was it a holiday job; still they succeeded.

And while they were at this work, which was difficult, their wives put in the night spending the money, which was easy. During that one night the nineteen wives spent an average of seven thousand dollars each out of the forty thousand in the sack—a hundred and thirty-three thousand altogether.

Next day there was a surprise for Jack Halliday. He noticed that the faces of the nineteen chief citizens and their wives bore that expression of peaceful and holy happiness again. He could not understand it, neither was he able to invent any remarks about it that could damage it or disturb it. And so it was his turn to be dissatisfied with life. His private guesses at the reasons for the happiness failed in all instances, upon examination. When he met Mrs. Wilcox and noticed the placid ecstasy in her face, he said to himself, "Her cat has had kittens"—and went and asked the cook; it was not so, the cook had detected the happiness, but did not know the cause. When Halliday found the duplicate ecstasy in the face of "Shadbelly" Billson (village nickname), he was sure some neighbor of Billson's had broken his leg, but inquiry showed that this had not happened. The subdued ecstasy in Gregory Yates's face could mean but one thing—he was a mother-in-law short; it was another mistake. "And Pinkerton—Pinkerton—he has collected ten cents that he thought he was going to lose." And so on, and so on. In some cases the guesses had to remain in doubt, in the others they proved distinct errors. In the end Halliday said to himself, "Anyway it foots up that there's nineteen Hadleyburg families temporarily in heaven: I don't know how it happened; I only know Providence is off duty to-day."

An architect and builder from the next State had lately ventured to set up a small business in this unpromising village, and his sign had now been hanging out a week. Not a customer yet; he was a discouraged man, and sorry he had come. But his weather changed suddenly now. First one and then another chief citizen's wife said to him privately:

"Come to my house Monday week—but say nothing about it for the present. We think of building."

He got eleven invitations that day. That night he wrote his daughter and broke off her match with her student. He said she could marry a mile higher than that.

Pinkerton the banker and two or three other well-to-do men planned country-seats—but waited. That kind don't count their chickens until they are hatched.

The Wilsons devised a grand new thing—a fancy-dress ball. They made no actual promises, but told all their acquaintanceship in confidence that they were thinking—the matter over and thought they should give it—"and if we do, you will be invited, of course." People were surprised, and said, one to another, "Why, they are crazy, those poor Wilsons, they can't afford it." Several among the nineteen said privately to their husbands, "It is a good idea, we will keep still till their cheap thing is over, then *we* will give one that will make it sick."

The days drifted along, and the bill of future squanderings rose higher and higher, wilder and wilder, more and more foolish and reckless. It began to look as if every member of the nineteen would not only spend his whole forty thousand dollars before receiving-day, but be actually in debt by the time he got the money. In some cases light-headed people did not stop with planning to spend, they really spent—on credit. They bought land, mortgages, farms, speculative stocks, fine clothes, horses, and various other things, paid down the bonus, and made themselves liable for the rest—at ten days. Presently the sober second thought came, and Halliday noticed that a ghastly anxiety was beginning to show up in a good many faces. Again he was puzzled, and didn't know what to make of it. "The Wilcox kittens aren't dead, for they weren't born; nobody's broken a leg; there's no shrinkage in mother-in-laws; *nothing* has happened—it is an unsolvable mystery."

There was another puzzled man, too—the Rev. Mr. Burgess. For days, wherever he went, people seemed to follow him or to be watching out for him; and if he ever found himself in a retired spot, a member of the nineteen would be sure to appear, thrust an envelope privately into his hand, whisper "To be opened at the town-hall Friday evening," then vanish away like a guilty thing. He was expecting that there might be one claimant for the sack—doubtful, however, Goodson being dead—but it never occurred to him that all this crowd might be claimants. When the great Friday came at last, he found that he had nineteen envelopes.

III

The town-hall had never looked finer. The platform at the end of it was backed by a showy draping of flags; at intervals along the walls were festoons of flags; the gallery fronts were clothed in flags; the supporting columns were swathed in flags; all this was to impress the stranger, for he would be there in considerable force, and in a large degree he would be connected with the press. The house was full. The 412 fixed seats were occupied; also the 68 extra chairs which had been packed into the aisles; the steps of the platform were occupied; some distinguished strangers were given seats on the platform; at the horseshoe of tables which fenced the front and sides of the platform sat a strong force of special correspondents who had come from everywhere. It was the best-dressed house the town had ever produced. There were some tolerably expensive toilets there, and in several cases the ladies who wore them had the look of being unfamiliar with that kind of clothes. At least the town thought they had that look, but the notion could have arisen from the town's knowledge of the fact that these ladies had never inhabited such clothes before.

The gold-sack stood on a little table at the front of the platform where all the house could see it. The bulk of the house gazed at it with a burning interest, a mouth-watering interest, a wistful and pathetic interest; a minority of nineteen couples gazed at it tenderly, lovingly, proprietarily, and the male half of this minority kept saying over to themselves the moving little impromptu speeches of thankfulness for the audience's applause and congratulations which they were presently going to get up and deliver. Every now and then one of these got a piece of paper out of his vest pocket and privately glanced at it to refresh his memory.

Of course there was a buzz of conversation going on—there always is; but at last, when the Rev. Mr. Burgess rose and laid his hand on the sack, he could hear his microbes gnaw, the place was so still. He related the curious history of the sack, then went on to speak in warm terms of Hadleyburg's old and well-earned reputation for spotless honesty, and of the town's just pride in this reputation. He said that this reputation was a treasure of priceless value; that under Providence its value had now become inestimably enhanced, for the recent episode had spread this fame far and wide, and thus had focused the eyes of the American world upon this village, and made its name for all time, as he hoped and believed, a synonym for commercial incorruptibility. [*Applause.*] "And who is to be the guardian of this noble fame—the community as a whole? No! The responsibility is individual, not communal. From this day forth each and every one of you is in his own person its special guardian, and individually responsible that no harm shall come to it. Do you—does each of you—accept this great trust? [*Tumultuous assent.*] Then all is well. Transmit it to your children and to your children's children. To-day your purity is beyond reproach—see to it that it shall remain so. To-day there is not a person in your community who could be beguiled to touch a penny not his own—see to it that you abide in this grace. [*"We will! we will!"*] This is not the place to make comparisons between ourselves and other communities—some of them ungracious towards us; they have their ways, we have ours; let us be content. [*Applause.*] I am done. Under my hand, my friends, rests a stranger's eloquent recognition of what we are; through him the world will always henceforth know what we are. We do not know who he is, but in your name I utter your gratitude, and ask you to raise your voices in indorsement."

The house rose in a body and made the walls quake with the thunders of its thankfulness for the space of a long minute. Then it sat down, and Mr. Burgess took an envelope out of his pocket. The house held its breath while he slit the envelope open and took from it a slip of paper. He read its contents—slowly and impressively—the audience listening with tranced attention to this magic document, each of whose words stood for an ingot of gold:

"'The remark which I made to the distressed stranger was this: 'You are very far from being a bad man; go, and reform.' Then he continued:

"We shall know in a moment now whether the remark here quoted corresponds with the one concealed in the sack; and if that shall prove to be so—and it undoubtedly will—this sack of gold belongs to a fellow-citizen who will henceforth stand before the nation as the symbol of the special virtue which has made our town famous throughout the land—Mr. Billson!"

The house had gotten itself all ready to burst into the proper tornado of applause; but instead of doing it, it seemed stricken with a paralysis; there was a deep hush for a moment or two, then a wave of whispered murmurs swept the place—of about this tenor: "*Billson!* oh, come, this is *too* thin! Twenty dollars to a stranger—or *anybody*—*Billson*! Tell it to the marines!" And now at this point the house caught its breath all of a sudden in a new access of astonishment, for it discovered that whereas in one part of the hall Deacon Billson was standing up with his head meekly bowed, in another part of it Lawyer Wilson was doing the same. There was a wondering silence now for a while.

Everybody was puzzled, and nineteen couples were surprised and indignant.

Billson and Wilson turned and stared at each other. Billson asked, bitingly:

"Why do *you* rise, Mr. Wilson?"

"Because I have a right to. Perhaps you will be good enough to explain to the house why *you* rise."

"With great pleasure. Because I wrote that paper."

"It is an impudent falsity! I wrote it myself."

It was Burgess's turn to be paralyzed. He stood looking vacantly at first one of the men and then the other, and did not seem to know what to do. The house was stupefied. Lawyer Wilson spoke up, now, and said:

"I ask the Chair to read the name signed to that paper."

That brought the Chair to itself, and it read out the name:

"John Wharton *Billson.*"

"There!" shouted Billson, "what have you got to say for yourself now? And what kind of apology are you going to make to me and to this insulted house for the imposture which you have attempted to play here?"

"No apologies are due, sir; and as for the rest of it, I publicly charge you with pilfering my note from Mr. Burgess and substituting a copy of it signed with your own name. There is no other way by which you could have gotten hold of the test-remark; I alone, of living men, possessed the secret of its wording."

There was likely to be a scandalous state of things if this went on; everybody noticed with distress that the shorthand scribes were scribbling like mad; many people were crying "Chair, chair! Order! order!" Burgess rapped with his gavel, and said:

"Let us not forget the proprieties due. There has evidently been a mistake somewhere, but surely that is all. If Mr. Wilson gave me an envelope—and I remember now that he did—I still have it."

He took one out of his pocket, opened it, glanced at it, looked surprised and worried, and stood silent a few moments. Then he waved his hand in a wandering and mechanical way, and made an effort or two to say something, then gave it up, despondently. Several voices cried out:

"Read it! read it! What is it?"

So he began, in a dazed and sleep-walker fashion:

"'The remark which I made to the unhappy stranger was this: "You are far from being a bad man. [The house gazed at him marvelling.] Go, and reform."' [*Murmurs:* "Amazing! what can this mean?"] This one," said the Chair, "is signed Thurlow G. Wilson."

"There!" cried Wilson, "I reckon that settles it! I knew perfectly well my note was purloined."

"Purloined!" retorted Billson. "I'll let you know that neither you nor any man of your kidney must venture to—"

The Chair: "Order, gentlemen, order! Take your seats, both of you, please."

They obeyed, shaking their heads and grumbling angrily. The house was profoundly puzzled; it did not know what to do with this curious emergency. Presently Thompson got up. Thompson was the hatter. He would have liked to be a Nineteener; but such was not for him; his stock of hats was not considerable enough for the position. He said:

"Mr. Chairman, if I may be permitted to make a suggestion, can both of these gentlemen be right? I put it to you, sir, can both have happened to say the very same words to the stranger? It seems to me—"

The tanner got up and interrupted him. The tanner was a disgruntled man; he believed himself entitled to be a Nineteener, but he couldn't get recognition. It made him a little unpleasant in his ways and speech. Said he:

"Sho, *that's* not the point! That could happen—twice in a hundred years—but not the other thing. Neither of them gave the twenty dollars!" [*A ripple of applause.*]

Billson. "*I* did!"

Wilson. "*I* did!"

Then each accused the other of pilfering.

The Chair. "Order! Sit down, if you please—both of you. Neither of the notes has been out of my possession at any moment."

A Voice. "Good—that settles *that*!"

The Tanner. "Mr. Chairman, one thing is now plain: one of these men has been eavesdropping under the other one's bed, and filching family secrets. If it is not unparliamentary to suggest it, I will remark that both are equal to it. [*The Chair.* "Order! order!"] I withdraw the remark, sir, and will confine myself to suggesting that *if* one of them has overheard the other reveal the test-remark to his wife, we shall catch him now."

A Voice. "How?"

The Tanner. "Easily. The two have not quoted the remark in exactly the same words. You would have noticed that, if there hadn't been a considerable stretch of time and an exciting quarrel inserted between the two readings."

A Voice. "Name the difference."

The Tanner. "The word *very* is in Billson's note, and not in the other."

Many Voices. "That's so—he's right!"

The Tanner. "And so, if the Chair will examine the test-remark in the sack, we shall know which of these two frauds—[*The Chair.* "Order!"]—which of these two adventurers—[*The Chair.* "Order! order!"]—which of these two gentlemen—[*laughter and applause*]—is entitled to wear the belt as being the first dishonest blatherskite ever bred in this town—which he has dishonored, and which will be a sultry place for him from now out!" [*Vigorous applause.*]

Many Voices. "Open it!—open the sack!"

Mr. Burgess made a slit in the sack, slid his hand in, and brought out an envelope. In it were a couple of folded notes. He said:

"One of these is marked, 'Not to be examined until all written communications which have been addressed to the Chair—if any—shall have been read.' The other is marked *'The Test.'* Allow me. It is worded—to wit:

"'I do not require that the first half of the remark which was made to me by my benefactor shall be quoted with exactness, for it was not striking, and could be forgotten; but its closing fifteen words are quite striking, and I think easily rememberable; unless *these* shall be accurately reproduced, let the applicant be regarded as an impostor. My benefactor began by saying he seldom gave advice to anyone, but that it always bore the hall-mark of high value when he did give it. Then he said this—and it has never faded from my memory: *'You are far from being a bad man.'* "

Fifty Voices. "That settles it—the money's Wilson's! Wilson! Wilson! Speech! Speech!"

People jumped up and crowded around Wilson, wringing his hand and congratulating fervently—meantime the Chair was hammering with the gavel and shouting:

"Order, gentlemen! Order! Order! Let me finish reading, please." When quiet was restored, the reading was resumed—as follows:

"'Go, and reform—or, mark my words—some day, for your sins you will die and go to hell or Hadleyburg—try and make it the former.'"

A ghastly silence followed. First an angry cloud began to settle darkly upon the faces of the citizenship; after a pause the cloud began to rise, and a tickled expression tried to take its place; tried so hard that it was only kept under with great and painful difficulty; the reporters, the Brixtonites, and other strangers bent their heads down and shielded their faces with their hands, and managed to hold in by main strength and heroic courtesy. At this most inopportune time burst upon the stillness the roar of a solitary voice—Jack Halliday's:

"*That's* got the hall-mark on it!"

Then the house let go, strangers and all. Even Mr. Burgess's gravity broke down presently, then the audience considered itself officially absolved from all restraint, and it made the most of its privilege. It was a good long laugh, and a tempestuously wholehearted one, but it ceased at last—long enough for Mr. Burgess to try to resume, and for the people to get their eyes partially wiped; then it broke out again, and afterward yet again; then at last Burgess was able to get out these serious words:

"It is useless to try to disguise the fact—we find ourselves in the presence of a matter of grave import. It involves the honor of your town—it strikes at the town's good name. The difference of a single word between the test-remarks offered by Mr. Wilson and Mr. Billson was itself a serious thing, since it indicated that one or the other of these gentlemen had committed a theft—"

The two men were sitting limp, nerveless, crushed; but at these words both were electrified into movement, and started to get up.—

"Sit down!" said the Chair, sharply, and they obeyed. "That, as I have said, was a serious thing. And it was—but for only one of them. But the matter has become graver; for the honour of *both* is now in formidable peril. Shall I go even further, and say in inextricable peril? *Both* left out the crucial fifteen words." He paused. During several moments he allowed the pervading stillness to gather and deepen its impressive effects, then added: "There would seem to be but one way whereby this could happen. I ask these gentlemen—Was there *collusion?—agreement?"*

A low murmur sifted through the house; its import was, "He's got them both."

Billson was not used to emergencies; he sat in a helpless collapse. But Wilson was a lawyer. He struggled to his feet, pale and worried, and said:

"I ask the indulgence of the house while I explain this most painful matter. I am sorry to say what I am about to say, since it must inflict irreparable injury upon Mr. Billson, whom I have always esteemed and respected until now, and in whose invulnerability to temptation I entirely believed—as did you all. But for the preservation of my own honor I must speak—and with frankness. I confess with shame—and I now beseech your pardon for it—that I said to the ruined stranger all of the words contained in the test-remark, including the disparaging fifteen. [*Sensation.*] When the late publication was made I recalled them, and I resolved to claim the sack of coin, for by every right I was entitled to it. Now I will ask you to consider this point, and weigh it well; that stranger's gratitude to me that night knew no bounds; he said himself that he could find no words for it that were adequate, and that if he should ever be able he would repay me a thousandfold. Now, then, I ask you this; could I expect—could I believe—could I even remotely imagine—that, feeling as he did, he would do so ungrateful a thing as to add those quite unnecessary fifteen words to his test?—set a trap for me?—expose me as a slanderer of my own town before my own people assembled in a public hall? It was preposterous; it was impossible. His test would contain only the kindly opening clause of my remark. Of that I had no shadow of doubt. You would have thought as I did. You would not have expected a base betrayal from one whom you had befriended and against whom you had committed no offense. And so with perfect confidence, perfect trust, I wrote on a piece of paper the opening words—ending with 'Go, and reform,'—and signed it. When I was about to put it in an envelope I was called into my back office, and without thinking I left the paper lying open on my desk." He stopped, turned his head slowly toward Billson, waited a moment, then added: "I ask you to note this; when I returned, a little latter, Mr. Billson was retiring by my street door." [*Sensation.*]

In a moment Billson was on his feet and shouting:

"It's a lie! It's an infamous lie!"

The Chair. "Be seated, sir! Mr. Wilson has the floor."

Billson's friends pulled him into his seat and quieted him, and Wilson went on:

"Those are the simple facts. My note was now lying in a different place on the table from where I had left it. I noticed that, but attached no importance to it, thinking a draught had blown it there. That Mr. Billson would read a private paper was a thing which could not occur to me; he was an honorable man, and he would be above that. If you will allow me to say it, I think his extra word *'very'* stands explained: it is attributable to a defect of memory. I was the only man in the world who could furnish here any detail of the test-mark—by *honorable* means. I have finished."

There is nothing in the world like a persuasive speech to fuddle the mental apparatus and upset the convictions and debauch the emotions of an audience not practised in the tricks and delusions of oratory. Wilson sat down victorious. The house submerged him in tides of approving applause; friends swarmed to him and shook him by the hand and congratulated him, and Billson was shouted down and not allowed to say a word. The Chair hammered and hammered with its gavel, and kept shouting:

"But let us proceed, gentlemen, let us proceed!"

At last there was a measurable degree of quiet, and the hatter said:

"But what is there to proceed with, sir, but to deliver the money?"

Voices. "That's it! That's it! Come forward, Wilson!"

The Hatter. "I move three cheers for Mr. Wilson, Symbol of the special virtue which—"

The cheers burst forth before he could finish; and in the midst of them—and in the midst of the clamor of the gavel also—some enthusiasts mounted Wilson on a big friend's shoulder and were going to fetch him in triumph to the platform. The Chair's voice now rose above the noise:

"Order! To your places! You forget that there is still a document to be read." When quiet had been restored he took up the document, and was going to read it, but laid it down again saying "I forgot; this is not to be read until all written communications received by me have first been read." He took an envelope out of his pocket, removed its inclosure, glanced at it—seemed astonished—held it out and gazed at it—stared at it.

Twenty or thirty voices cried out:

"What is it? Read it! read it!"

And he did—slowly, and wondering:

"'The remark which I made to the stranger—[*Voices.* "Hello! how's this?"]—was this: 'You are far from being a bad man. [*Voices.* "Great Scott!"] Go, and reform.'" [*Voices.* "Oh, saw my leg off!"] Signed by Mr. Pinkerton the banker."

The pandemonium of delight which turned itself loose now was of a sort to make the judicious weep. Those whose withers were unwrung laughed till the tears ran down; the reporters, in throes of laughter, set down disordered pot-hooks which would never in the world be decipherable; and a sleeping dog jumped up scared out of its wits, and barked itself crazy at the turmoil. All manner of cries were scattered through the din: "We're getting rich—*two* Symbols of Incorruptibility!—without counting Billson!" "*Three!*—count Shadbelly in—we can't have too many!" "All right—Billson's elected!" "Alas, poor Wilson! victim of *two* thieves!"

A Powerful Voice. "Silence! The Chair's fished up something more out of its pocket."

Voices. "Hurrah! Is it something fresh? Read it! read! read!"

The Chair [*reading*]. "'The remark which I made,' etc. 'You are far from being a bad man. Go,' etc. Signed, 'Gregory Yates.'"

Tornado of Voices. "Four Symbols!" "'Rah for Yates!" "Fish again!"

The house was in a roaring humor now, and ready to get all the fun out of the occasion that might be in it. Several Nineteeners, looking pale and distressed, got up and began to work their way towards the aisles, but a score of shouts went up:

"The doors, the doors—close the doors; no Incorruptible shall leave this place! Sit down, everybody!" The mandate was obeyed.

"Fish again! Read! read!"

The Chair fished again, and once more the familiar words began to fall from its lips—"'You are far from being a bad man—'"

"Name! name! What's his name?"

"'L. Ingoldsby Sargent.'"

"Five elected! Pile up the Symbols! Go on, go on!"

"'You are far from being a bad—'"

"Name! name!"

"'Nicholas Whitworth.'"

"Hooray! hooray! it's a symbolical day!"

Somebody wailed in, and began to sing this rhyme (leaving out "it's") to the lovely "Mikado" tune of "When a man's afraid, a beautiful maid;" the audience joined in, with joy; then, just in time, somebody contributed another line—

"And don't you this forget—"

The house roared it out. A third line was at once furnished—

"Corruptibles far from Hadleyburg are—"

The house roared that one too. As the last note died, Jack Halliday's voice rose high and clear, freighted with a final line—

"But the Symbols are here, you bet!"

That was sung, with booming enthusiasm. Then the happy house started in at the beginning and sang the four lines through twice, with immense swing and dash, and finished up with a crashing three-times-three and a tiger for "Hadleyburg the Incorruptible and all Symbols of it which we shall find worthy to receive the hall-mark to-night."

Then the shoutings at the Chair began again, all over the place:

"Go on! go on! Read! read some more! Read all you've got!"

"That's it—go on! We are winning eternal celebrity!"

A dozen men got up now and began to protest. They said that this farce was the work of some abandoned joker, and was an insult to the whole community. Without a doubt these signatures were all forgeries—

"Sit down! sit down! Shut up! You are confessing. We'll find *your* names in the lot."

"Mr. Chairman, how many of those envelopes have you got?"

The Chair counted.

"Together with those that have been already examined, there are nineteen."

A storm of derisive applause broke out.

"Perhaps they all contain the secret. I move that you open them all and read every signature that is attached to a note of that sort—and read also the first eight words of the note."

"Second the motion!"

It was put and carried—uproariously. Then poor old Richards got up, and his wife rose and stood at his side. Her head was bent down, so that none might see that she was crying. Her husband gave her his arm, and so supporting her, he began to speak in a quavering voice:

"My friends, you have known us two—Mary and me—all our lives, and I think you have liked us and respected us—"

The Chair interrupted him:

"Allow me. It is quite true—that which you are saying, Mr. Richards; this town *does* know you two; it *does* like you; it *does* respect you; more—it honors you and *loves* you—"

Halliday's voice rang out:

"That's the hall-marked truth, too! If the Chair is right, let the house speak up and say it. Rise! Now, then—hip! hip! hip!—all together!"

The house rose in mass, faced toward the old couple eagerly, filled the air with a snow-storm of waving handkerchiefs, and delivered the cheers with all its affectionate heart.

The Chair then continued:

"What I was going to say is this: We know your good heart, Mr. Richards, but this is not a time for the exercise of charity toward offenders. [*Shouts of "Right! right!"*] I see your generous purpose in your face, but I cannot allow you to plead for these men—"

"But I was going to—"

"Please take your seat, Mr. Richards. We must examine the rest of these notes—simple fairness to the men who have already been exposed requires this. As soon as that has been done—I give you my word for this—you shall he heard."

Many voices. "Right!—the Chair is right—no interruption can be permitted at this stage! Go on!—the names! the names!—according to the terms of the motion!"

The old couple sat reluctantly down, and the husband whispered to the wife, "It is pitifully hard to have to wait; the shame will be greater than ever when they find we were only going to plead for *ouselves*."

Straightway the jollity broke loose again with the reading of the names.

"'You are far from being a bad man—' Signature, 'Robert J. Titmarsh.'"

'"You are far from being a bad man—' Signature, 'Eliphalet Weeks.'"

"'You are far from being a bad man—' Signature, 'Oscar B. Wilder.'"

At this point the house lit upon the idea of taking the eight words out of the Chairman's hands. He was not unthankful for that. Thenceforward he held up each note in its turn and waited. The house droned out the eight words in a massed and measured and musical deep volume of sound (with a daringly close resemblance to a well-known church chant)—"You are f-a-r from being a b-a-a-a-d man." Then the Chair said, "Signature, 'Archibald Wilcox.'" And so on, and so on, name after name, and everybody had an increasingly and gloriously good time except the wretched Nineteen. Now and then, when a particularly shining name was called, the house made the Chair wait while it chanted the whole of the test-remark from the beginning to the closing words, "And go to hell or Hadleyburg—try and make it the for-or-m-e-r!" and in these special cases they added a grand and agonised and imposing "A-a-a-a-*men*!"

The list dwindled, dwindled, dwindled, poor old Richards keeping tally of the count, wincing when a name resembling his own was pronounced, and waiting in miserable suspense for the time to come when it would be his humiliating privilege to rise with Mary and finish his plea, which he was intending to word thus: ". . . for until now we have never done any wrong thing, but have gone our humble way unreproached. We are very poor, we are old, and, have no chick nor child to help us; we were sorely tempted, and we fell. It was my purpose when I got up before to make confession and beg that my name might not be read out in this public place, for it seemed to us that we could not bear it; but I was prevented. It was just; it was our place to suffer with the rest. It has been hard for us. It is the first time we have ever heard our name fall from any one's lips—sullied. Be merciful—for the sake or the better days; make our shame as light to bear as in your charity you can." At this point in his reverie Mary nudged him, perceiving that his mind was absent. The house was chanting, "You are f-a-r," etc.

"Be ready," Mary whispered. "Your name comes now; he has read eighteen."

The chant ended.

"Next! next! next!" came volleying from all over the house.

Burgess put his hand into his pocket. The old couple, trembling, began to rise. Burgess fumbled a moment, then said:

"I find I have read them all."

Faint with joy and surprise, the couple sank into their seats, and Mary whispered:

"Oh, bless God, we are saved!—he has lost ours—I wouldn't give this for a hundred of those sacks!"

The house burst out with its "Mikado" travesty, and sang it three times with ever-increasing enthusiasm, rising to its feet when it reached for the third time the closing line—

"But the Symbols are here, you bet!"

and finishing up with cheers and a tiger for "Hadleyburg purity and our eighteen immortal representatives of it."

Then Wingate, the saddler, got up and proposed cheers "for the cleanest man in town, the one solitary important citizen in it who didn't try to steal that money—Edward Richards."

They were given with great and moving heartiness; then somebody proposed that "Richards be elected sole Guardian and Symbol of the now Sacred Hadleyburg Tradition, with power and right to stand up and look the whole sarcastic world in the face."

Passed, by acclamation; then they sang the "Mikado" again, and ended it with—

"And there's *one* Symbol left, you bet!"

There was a pause; then—

A Voice. "Now, then, who's to get the sack?"

The Tanner (*with bitter sarcasm*). "That's easy. The money has to be divided among the eighteen Incorruptibles. They gave the suffering stranger twenty dollars apiece—and that remark—each in his turn—it took twenty-two minutes for the procession to move past. Staked the stranger—total contribution, $360. All they want is just the loan back—and interest—forty thousand dollars altogether."

Many Voices [*derisively.*] "That's it! Divvy! divvy! Be kind to the poor—don't keep them waiting!"

The Chair. "Order! I now offer the stranger's remaining document. It says: 'If no claimant shall appear [*grand chorus of groans*], I desire that you open the sack and count out the money to the principal citizens of your town, they to take it in trust [*Cries of "Oh! Oh! Oh!"*], and use it in such ways as to them shall seem best for the propagation and preservation of your community's noble reputation for incorruptible honesty [*more cries*]—a reputation to which their names and their efforts will add a new and far-reaching luster." [*Enthusiastic outburst of sarcastic applause.*] That seems to be all. No—here is a postscript:

"'*P.S.—CITIZENS OF HADLEYBURG: There IS no test-remark—nobody made one.* [Great sensation.] *There wasn't any pauper stranger, nor any twenty-dollar contribution, nor any accompanying benediction and compliment—these are all inventions.* [General buzz and hum of astonishment and delight.] *Allow me to tell my story—it will take but a word or two. I passed through your town at a certain time, and received a deep offence which I had not earned. Any other man would have been content to kill one or two of you and call it square, but to me that would have been a trivial revenge, and inadequate; for the dead do not* suffer. *Besides I could not kill you all—and, anyway, made as I am, even that would not have satisfied me. I wanted to damage every man in the place, and every woman—and not in their bodies or in their estate, but in their vanity—the place where feeble and foolish people are most vulnerable. So I disguised myself and came back and studied you. You were easy game. You had an old and lofty reputation for honesty, and naturally you were proud of it—it was your treasure of treasures, the very apple of your eye. As soon as I found out that you carefully and vigilantly kept yourselves and your children* out of temptation, *I knew how to proceed. Why, you simple creatures, the weakest of all weak things is a virtue which has not been tested in the fire. I laid a plan, and gathered a list of names. My project was to corrupt Hadleyburg the Incorruptible. My idea was to make liars and thieves of nearly half a hundred smirchless men and women who had never in their lives uttered a lie or stolen a penny. I was afraid of Goodson. He was neither born nor reared in Hadleyburg. I was afraid that if I started to operate my scheme by getting my letter laid before you, you would say to yourselves, 'Goodson is the only man among us who would give away twenty dollars to a poor devil'—and then you might not bite at my bait. But heaven took Goodson; then I knew I was safe, and I set my trap and baited it. It may be that I shall not catch all the men to whom I mailed the pretended test-secret, but I shall catch the most of them, if I know Hadleyburg nature.* [Voices. "Right—he got every last one of them."] *I believe they will even steal ostensible* gamble-*money, rather than miss, poor, tempted, and mistrained fellows. I am hoping to eternally and everlastingly squelch your vanity and give Hadleyburg a new renown—one that will* stick*—and spread far. If I have succeeded, open the sack and summon the Committee on Propagation and Preservation of the Hadleyburg Reputation.'"*

A Cyclone of Voices. "Open it! Open it! The Eighteen to the front! Committee on Propagation of the Tradition! Forward—the Incorruptibles!"

The Chair ripped the sack wide, and gathered up a handful of bright, broad, yellow coins, shook them together, then examined them.

"Friends, they are only gilded disks of lead!"

There was a crashing outbreak of delight over this news, and when the noise had subsided, the tanner called out:

"By right of apparent seniority in this business, Mr. Wilson is Chairman of the Committee on Propagation of the Tradition. I suggest that he step forward on behalf of his pals, and receive in trust the money."

A Hundred Voices. "Wilson! Wilson! Wilson! Speech! Speech!"

Wilson [*in a voice trembling with anger*]. "You will allow me to say, and without apologies for my language, *damn* the money!"

A Voice. "Oh, and him a Baptist!"

A Voice. "Seventeen Symbols left! Step up, gentlemen, and assume your trust!"

There was a pause—no response.

The Saddler. "Mr. Chairman, we've got *one* clean man left, anyway, out of the late aristocracy; and he needs money, and deserves it. I move that you appoint Jack Halliday to get up there and auction off that sack of gilt twenty-dollar pieces, and give the result to the right man—the man whom Hadleyburg delights to honour—Edward Richards."

This was received with great enthusiasm, the dog taking a hand again; the saddler started the bids at a dollar, the Brixton folk and Barnum's representative fought hard for it, the people cheered every jump that the bids made, the excitement climbed moment by moment higher and higher, the bidders got on their mettle and grew steadily more and more daring, more and more determined, the jumps went from a dollar up to five, then to ten, then to twenty, then fifty, then to a hundred, then—

At the beginning of the auction Richards whispered in distress to his wife: "Oh, Mary, can we allow it? It—it—you see, it is an honor—reward, a testimonial to purity of character, and—and—can we allow it? Hadn't I better get up and—Oh, Mary, what ought we to do?—what do you think we—" [*Halliday's voice. "Fifteen I'm bid!—fifteen for the sack!—twenty!—ah, thanks!—thirty—thanks again! Thirty, thirty, thirty!—do I hear forty?—forty it is! Keep the ball rolling, gentlemen, keep it rolling!—fifty!—thanks, noble Roman!—going at fifty, fifty, fifty!—seventy!—ninety!—splendid!—a hundred!—pile it up, pile it up—hundred and twenty—forty—just in time!—hundred and fifty!—Two hundred!—superb! Do I hear two h—thanks!—two hundred and fifty!—"*]

"It is another temptation, Edward—I'm all in a tremble—but, oh, we've escaped *one* temptation, and that ought to warn us, to—[*"Six did I hear?—thanks!—six fifty, six f—SEVEN hundred!"*] And yet, Edward, when you think—nobody susp—[*"Eight hundred dollars!—hurrah!—make it nine!—Mr. Parsons, did I hear you say—thanks!—nine!—this noble sack of virgin lead going at only nine hundred dollars, gilding and all—come! do I hear—a thousand!—gratefully yours!—did some one say eleven?—a sack which is going to be the most celebrated in the whole Uni—"*] "Oh, Edward" (beginning to sob), "we are so poor!—but—but—do as you think best—do as you think best."

Edward fell—that is, he sat still; sat with a conscience which was not satisfied, but which was overpowered by circumstances.

Meantime a stranger, who looked like an amateur detective gotten up as an impossible English earl, had been watching the evening's proceedings with manifest interest, and with a contented expression in his face; and he had been privately commenting to himself. He was now soliloquizing somewhat like this: 'None of the Eighteen are bidding; that is not satisfactory; I must change that—the dramatic unities require it; they must buy the sack they tried to steal; they must pay a heavy price, too—some of them are rich. And another thing, when I make a mistake in Hadleyburg nature the man that puts that error upon me is entitled to a high honorarium, and some one must pay. This poor old Richards has brought my judgment to shame; he is an honest man:—I don't understand it, but I acknowledge it. Yes, he saw my deuces—*and* with a straight flush, and by rights the pot is his. And it shall be a jack-pot, too, if I can manage it. He disappointed me, but let that pass."

He was watching the bidding. At a thousand, the market broke: the prices tumbled swiftly. He waited—and still watched. One competitor dropped out; then another, and another. He put in a bid or two now. When the bids had sunk to ten dollars, he added a five; some one raised him a three; he waited a moment, then flung in a fifty-dollar jump, and the sack was his—at $1,282. The house broke out in cheers—then stopped; for he was on his feet, and had lifted his hand. He began to speak.

"I desire to say a word, and ask a favour. I am a speculator in rarities, and I have dealings with persons interested in numismatics all over the world. I can make a profit on this purchase, just as it stands; but there is a way, if I can get your approval, whereby I can make every one of these leaden twenty-dollar pieces worth its face in gold, and perhaps more. Grant me that approval, and I will give part of my gains to your Mr. Richards, whose invulnerable probity you have so justly and so cordially recognised tonight; his share shall be ten thousand dollars, and I will hand him the money to-morrow. [*Great applause from the house.* But the "invulnerable probity" made the Richardses blush prettily; however, it went for modesty, and did no harm.] If you will pass my proposition by a good majority—I would like a two-thirds vote—I will regard that as the town's consent, and that is all I ask. Rarities are always helped by any device which will rouse curiosity and compel remark. Now if I may have your permission to stamp upon the faces of each of these ostensible coins the names of the eighteen gentlemen who—"

Nine-tenths of the audience were on their feet in a moment—dog and all—and the proposition was carried with a whirlwind of approving applause and laughter.

They sat down, and all the Symbols except "Dr." Clay Harkness got up, violently protesting against the proposed outrage, and threatening to—

"I beg you not to threaten me," said the stranger calmly. "I know my legal rights, and am not accustomed to being frightened at bluster." [*Applause.*] He sat down. "Dr." Harkness saw an opportunity here. He was one of the two very rich men of the place, and Pinkerton was the other. Harkness was proprietor of a mint; that is to say, a popular patent medicine. He was running for the Legislature on one ticket, and Pinkerton on the other. It was a close race and a hot one, and getting hotter every day. Both had strong appetites for money; each had bought a great tract of land, with a purpose; there was going to be a new railway, and each wanted to be in the Legislature and help locate the route to his own advantage; a single vote might make the decision, and with it two or three fortunes. The stake was large, and Harkness was a daring speculator. He was sitting close to the stranger. He leaned over while one or another of the other Symbols was entertaining the house with protests and appeals, and asked, in a whisper,

"What is your price for the sack?"

"Forty thousand dollars."

"I'll give you twenty."

"No."

"Twenty-five."

"No."

"Say thirty."

"The price is forty thousand dollars; not a penny less."

"All right, I'll give it. I will come to the hotel at ten in the morning. I don't want it known; will see you privately."

"Very good." Then the stranger got up and said to the house:

"I find it late. The speeches of these gentlemen are not without merit, not without interest, not without grace; yet if I may he excused I will take my leave. I thank you for the great favour which you have shown me in granting my petition. I ask the Chair to keep the sack for me until to-morrow, and to hand these three five-hundred-dollar notes to Mr. Richards." They were passed up to the Chair.

"At nine I will call for the sack, and at eleven will deliver the rest of the ten thousand to Mr. Richards in person at his home. Good-night."

Then he slipped out, and left the audience making a vast noise, which was composed of a mixture of cheers, the "Mikado" song, dog-disapproval, and the chant, "You are f-a-r from being a b-a-a-d man—a-a-a a-men!"

IV

At home the Richardses had to endure congratulations and compliments until midnight. Then they were left to themselves. They looked a little sad, and they sat silent and thinking. Finally Mary sighed and said:

"Do you think we are to blame, Edward—*much* to blame?" and her eyes wandered to the accusing triplet of big bank-notes lying on the table, where the congratulators had been gloating over them and reverently fingering them. Edward did not answer at once; then he brought out a sigh and said, hesitatingly:

"We—we couldn't help it, Mary. It—well it was ordered. *All* things are."

Mary glanced up and looked at him steadily, but he didn't return the look. Presently she said:

"I thought congratulations and praises always tasted good. But—it seems to me, now—Edward?"

"Well?"

"Are you going to stay in the bank?"

"N-no."

"Resign?"

"In the morning—by note."

"It does seem best."

Richards bowed his head in his hands and muttered:

"Before, I was not afraid to let oceans of people's money pour through my hands, but—Mary, I am so tired, so tired—"

"We will go to bed."

At nine in the morning the stranger called for the sack and took it to the hotel in a cab. At ten Harkness had a talk with him privately. The stranger asked for and got five checks on a metropolitan bank—drawn to "Bearer,"—four for $1,500 each, and one for $34,000. He put one of the former in his pocket-book, and the remainder, representing $38,500, he put in an envelope, and with these he added a note, which he wrote after Harkness was gone. At eleven he called at the Richards house and knocked. Mrs. Richards peeped through the shutters, then went and received the envelope, and the stranger disappeared without a word. She came back flushed and a little unsteady on her legs, and gasped out:

"I am sure I recognized him! Last night it seemed to me that maybe I had seen him somewhere before."

"He is the man that brought the sack here?"

"I am almost sure of it."

"Then he is the ostensible Stephenson, too, and sold every important citizen in this town with his bogus secret. Now if he has sent checks instead of money, we are sold too, after we thought we had escaped. I was beginning to feel fairly comfortable once more, after my night's rest, but the look of that envelope makes me sick. It isn't fat enough; $8,500 in even the largest bank-notes makes more bulk than that."

"Edward, why do you object to checks?"

"Checks signed by Stephenson! I am resigned to take the $8,500 if it could come in bank-notes—for it does seem that it was so ordered, Mary—but I have never had much courage, and I have not the pluck to try to market a check signed with that disastrous name. It would be a trap. That man tried to catch me; we escaped somehow or other; and now he is trying a new way. If it is checks—"

"Oh, Edward, it is *too* bad!" And she held up the checks and began to cry.

"Put them in the fire! quick! we mustn't be tempted. It is a trick to make the world laugh at *us,* along with the rest, and—Give them to *me,* since you can't do it!" He snatched them and tried to hold his grip till he could get to the stove; but he was human, he was a cashier, and he stopped a moment to make sure of the signature. Then he came near to fainting.

"Fan me, Mary, fan me! They are the same as gold!"

"Oh, how lovely, Edward! Why?"

"Signed by Harkness. What can the mystery of that be, Mary?"

"Edward, do you think—"

"Look here—look at this! Fifteen—fifteen—fifteen—thirty-four. Thirty-eight thousand five hundred! Mary, the sack isn't worth twelve dollars, and Harkness—apparently—has paid about par for it."

"And does it all come to us, do you think—instead of the ten thousand?"

"Why, it looks like it. And the checks are made to 'Bearer,' too."

"Is that good, Edward? What is it for?"

"A hint to collect them at some distant bank, I reckon. Perhaps Harkness doesn't want the matter known. What is that—a note?"

"Yes. It was with the checks."

It was in the "Stephenson" handwriting, but there was no signature. It said:

I am a disappointed man. Your honesty is beyond the reach of temptation. I had a different idea about it, but I wronged you in that, and I beg pardon, and do it sincerely. I honour you—and that is sincere too. This town is not worthy to kiss the hem of your garment. Dear sir, I made a square bet with myself that there were nineteen debauchable men in your self-righteous community. I have lost. Take the whole pot, you are entitled to it.

Richards drew a deep sigh, and said:

"It seems written with fire—it burns so. Mary—I am miserable again."

"I, too. Ah, dear, I wish—"

"To think, Mary—he *believes* in me."

"Oh, don't, Edward—I can't bear it."

"If those beautiful words were deserved, Mary—and God knows I believed I deserved them once—I think I could give the forty thousand dollars for them. And I would put that paper away, as representing more than gold and jewels, and keep it always. But now—We could not live in the shadow of its accusing presence, Mary."

He put it in the fire.

A messenger arrived and delivered an envelope. Richards took from it a note and read it; it was from Burgess:

You saved me, in a difficult time. I saved you last night. It was at cost of a lie, but I made the sacrifice freely, and out of a grateful heart. None in this village knows so well as I know how brave and good and noble you are. At bottom you cannot respect me, knowing as you do of that matter of which I am accused, and by the general voice condemned; but I beg that you will at least believe that I am a grateful man; it will help me to bear my burden. [Signed] 'BURGESS.'

"Saved, once more. And on such terms!" He put the note in the fire. "I—I wish I were dead, Mary, I wish I were out of it all!"

"Oh, these are bitter, bitter days, Edward. The stabs, through their very generosity, are so deep—and they come so fast!"

Three days before the election each of two thousand voters suddenly found himself in possession of a prized memento—one of the renowned bogus double-eagles. Around one of its faces was stamped these words: "THE REMARK I MADE TO THE POOR STRANGER WAS—" Around the other face was stamped these: "GO, AND REFORM. [SIGNED] PINKERTON." Thus the entire remaining refuse of the renowned joke was emptied upon a single head, and with calamitous effect. It revived the recent vast laugh and concentrated it upon Pinkerton; and Harkness's election was a walk-over.

Within twenty-four hours after the Richardses had received their checks their consciences were quieting down, discouraged; the old couple were learning to reconcile themselves to the sin which they had committed. But they were to learn, now, that a sin takes on new and real terrors when there seems a chance that it is going to be found out. This gives it a fresh and most substantial and important aspect. At church the morning sermon was of the usual pattern; it was the same old things said in the same old way; they had heard them a thousand times and found them innocuous, next to meaningless, and easy to sleep under; but now it was different: the sermon seemed to bristle with accusations; it seemed aimed straight and specially at people who were concealing deadly sins. After church they got away from the mob of congratulators as soon as they could, and hurried homeward, chilled to the bone at they did not know what—vague, shadowy, indefinite fears. And by chance they caught a glimpse of Mr. Burgess as he turned a corner. He paid no attention to their nod of recognition! He hadn't seen it; but they did not know that. What could his conduct mean? It might mean—it might mean—oh, a dozen dreadful things. Was it possible that he knew that Richards could have cleared him of guilt in that bygone time, and had been silently waiting for a chance to even up accounts? At home, in their distress they got to imagining that their servant might have been in the next room listening when Richards revealed the secret to his wife that he knew of Burgess's innocence; next, Richards began to imagine that he had heard the swish of a gown in there at that time; next, he was sure he *had* heard it. They would call Sarah in, on a pretext, and watch her face; if she had been betraying them to Mr. Burgess, it would show in her manner. They asked her some questions—questions which were so random and incoherent and seemingly purposeless that the girl felt sure that the old people's minds had been affected by their sudden good fortune; the sharp and watchful gaze which they bent upon her frightened her, and that completed the business. She blushed, she became nervous and confused, and to the old people these were plain signs of guilt—guilt of some fearful sort or other—without doubt she was a spy and a traitor. When they were alone again they began to piece many unrelated things together and get horrible results out of the combination. When things had got about to the worst, Richards was delivered of a sudden gasp and his wife asked:

"Oh, what is it?—what is it?"

"The note—Burgess's note! Its language was sarcastic, I see it now." He quoted: "'At bottom you cannot respect me, *knowing,* as you do, of *that matter of* which I am accused'—oh, it is perfectly plain, now, God help me! He knows that I know! You see the ingenuity of the phrasing. It was a trap—and like a fool, I walked into it. And Mary—!"

"Oh, it is dreadful—I know what you are going to say—he didn't return your transcript of the pretended test-remark."

"No—kept it to destroy us with. Mary, he has exposed us to some already. I know it—I know it well. I saw it in a dozen faces after church. Ah, he wouldn't answer our nod of recognition—*he* knew what he had been doing!"

In the night the doctor was called. The news went around in the morning that the old couple were rather seriously ill—prostrated by the exhausting excitement growing out of their great windfall, the congratulations, and the late hours, the doctor said. The town was sincerely distressed; for these old people were about all it had left to be proud of, now.

Two days later the news was worse. The old couple were delirious, and were doing strange things. By witness of the nurses, Richards had exhibited checks—for $8,500? No—for an amazing sum—$38,500! What could be the explanation of this gigantic piece of luck?

The following day the nurses had more news—and wonderful. They had concluded to hide the checks, lest harm come to them; but when they searched they were gone from under the patient's pillow—vanished away. The patient said:

"Let the pillow alone; what do you want?"

"We thought it best that the checks—"

"You will never see them again—they are destroyed. They came from Satan. I saw the hell-brand on them, and I knew they were sent to betray me to sin." Then he fell to gabbling strange and dreadful things which were not clearly understandable, and which the doctor admonished them to keep to themselves.

Richards was right; the checks were never seen again.

A nurse must have talked in her sleep, for within two days the forbidden gabblings were the property of the town; and they were of a surprising sort. They seemed to indicate that Richards had been a claimant for the sack himself, and that Burgess had concealed that fact and then maliciously betrayed it.

Burgess was taxed with this and stoutly denied it. And he said it was not fair to attach weight to the chatter of a sick old man who was out of his mind. Still, suspicion was in the air, and there was much talk.

After a day or two it was reported that Mrs. Richards's delirious deliveries were getting to be duplicates of her husband's. Suspicion flamed up into conviction, now, and the town's pride in the purity of its one undiscredited important citizen began to dim down and flicker toward extinction.

Six days passed, then came more news. The old couple were dying. Richards's mind cleared in his latest hour, and he sent for Burgess. Burgess said:

"Let the room be cleared. I think he wishes to say something in privacy."

"No!" said Richards; "I want witnesses. I want you all to hear my confession, so that I may die a man, and not a dog. I was clean—artificially—like the rest; and like the rest I fell when temptation came. I signed a lie, and claimed the miserable sack. Mr. Burgess remembered that I had done him a service, and in gratitude (and ignorance) he suppressed my claim and saved me. You know the thing that was charged against Burgess years ago. My testimony, and mine alone, could have cleared him, and I was a coward and left him to suffer disgrace—"

"No—no—Mr. Richards, you—"

"My servant betrayed my secret to him—"

"No one has betrayed anything to me—"

"And then he did a natural and justifiable thing; he repented of the saving kindness which he had done me, and he *exposed* me—as I deserved—"

"Never!—I make oath—"

"Out of my heart I forgive him."

Burgess's impassioned protestations fell upon deaf ears; the dying man passed away without knowing that once more he had done poor Burgess a wrong. The old wife died that night. The last of the sacred Nineteen had fallen a prey to the fiendish sack; the town was stripped of the last rag of its ancient glory. Its mourning was not showy, but it was deep.

By act of the Legislature—upon prayer and petition—Hadleyburg was allowed to change its name to (never mind what—I will not give it away), and leave one word out of the motto that for many generations had graced the town's official seal.

It is an honest town once more, and the man will have to rise early that catches it napping again.

Happiness

Priscilla Leonard

Happiness is like a crystal,
Fair and exquisite and clear,
Broken in a million pieces,
Shattered, scattered far and near.
Now and then along life's pathway,
Lo! some shining fragments fall;
But there are so many pieces
No one ever finds them all.

You may find a bit of beauty,
Or an honest share of wealth,
While another just beside you
Fathers honor, love, or health.
Vain to choose or grasp unduly,
Broken is the perfect ball;
And there are so many pieces
No one ever finds them all.

Yet the wise as on they journey
Treasure every fragment clear,
Fit them as they may together,
Imaging the shattered sphere,
Learning ever to be thankful,
Though their share of it is small;
For it has so many pieces
No one ever finds them all.

From *Best Loved Poems to Read Again and Again.*

Before I Could Call Myself Ángel Gonzáles

Ángel Gonzáles
translated from the Spanish by Steven Ford Brown and Gutierrez Revuelta

Before I could call myself Ángel Gonzáles,
before the earth could support the weight of my body,
a long time
and a great space were necessary:
men from all the seas and all the lands,
fertile wombs of women, and bodies
and more bodies, incessantly fusing
into another new body.
Solstices and equinoxes illuminated
with their changing lights, and variegated skies,
the millenary trip of my flesh
as it climbed over centuries and bones.
Let me tell you
about yesterday, once more
about yesterday: the incomparable
day that no one will ever
see again upon the earth.

The Future

Ángel Gonzáles
translated from the Spanish by Steven Ford Brown and Gutierrez Revuelta

But the future is different
from that destiny seen from afar,
magical world, vast sphere
brushed by the long arm of desire,
brilliant ball the eyes dream,
shared dwelling
of hope and deception, dark
land
of illusion and tears
the stars predicted
and the heart awaits
and that is always, always, always distant.

But, I think, the future is also another thing:
a verb tense in motion, in action, in combat,
a searching movement toward life,
keel of the ship that strikes the water
and struggles to open between the waves
the exact breach the rudder commands.

I'm on this line, in this deep
trajectory of agony and battle,
trapped in a tunnel or trench
that with my hands I open, close, or leave,
obeying the heart that orders,
pushes, determines, demands, and searches.

Future of mine...! Distant heart
that dictated it yesterday:
don't be ashamed.
Today is the result of your blood,
pain that I recognize, light that I admit,
suffering that I assume,
love that I intend.

But still, nothing is definitive.
Tomorrow I have decided to go ahead
and advance,
tomorrow I am prepared to be content,
tomorrow I will love you, morning
and night,
tomorrow will not be exactly as God wishes.

Tomorrow, gray or luminous, or cold,
that hands shape in the wind,
that fists draw in the air.

Now That the Time Seems All Mine

Patrizia Cavalli
translated from the Italian by Judith Baumel

Now that time seems all mine
and no one calls me for lunch or dinner,
now that I can stay to watch
how a cloud loosens and loses its color,
how a cat walks on the roof
in the immense luxury of a prowl, now
that what waits for me every day
is the unlimited length of a night
where there is no call and no longer a reason
to undress in a hurry to rest inside
the blinding sweetness of a body that waits for me,
now that the morning no longer has a beginning
and silently leaves me to my plans,
to all the cadences of my voice, now
suddenly I would like prison.

Far from Kingdoms

Patrizia Cavalli
translated from the Italian by Judith Baumel

Far from kingdoms
how steady is the room!
Come, breathe close with me
so I may discover the sweetness
of many imperfections, some missing
tooth, some extra wrinkle, and your body
worn out slightly by carelessness.

Middle Class Blues

Hans Magnus Enzensberger

We can't complain.
We're not out of work.
We don't go hungry.
We eat.

The grass grows,
the social product,
the fingernail,
the past.

The streets are empty.
The deals are closed.
The sirens are silent.
All that will pass.

The dead have made their wills.
The rain's become a drizzle.
The war's not yet been declared.
There's no hurry for that.

We eat the grass.
We eat the social product.
We eat the fingernails.
We eat the past.

We have nothing to conceal.
We have nothing to miss.
We have nothing to say.
We have.

The watch has been wound up.
The bills have been paid.
The washing-up has been done.
Thc last bus is passing by.

It is empty.

We can't complain.

What are we waiting for?

Song for Those Who Know

Hans Magnus Enzensberger

Something must be done right away
that much we know
but of course it's too soon to act
but of course it's too late in the day
oh we know

we know that we're really rather well off
and that we'll go on like this
and that it's not much use anyway
oh we know

we know that we are to blame
and that it's not our fault if we are to blame
and that we're to blame for the fact that it's not our fault
and that we're fed up with it
oh we know

and that maybe it would be a good idea to keep our mouths shut
and that we won't keep our mouths shut all the same
oh we know
oh we know

and we also know that we can't help anybody really
and that nobody really can help us
oh we know

and that we're extremely gifted and brilliant
and free to choose between nothing and naught
and that we must analyse this problem very carefully
and that we take two lumps of sugar in our tea
oh we know

we know all about oppression
and that we are very much against it
and that cigarettes have gone up again
oh we know

From *Selected Poems* by Hans Magnus Enzensberger. Reprinted by permission of The Sheep Meadow Press.

we know very well that the nation is heading for real trouble
and that our forecasts have usually been dead right
and that they are not of any use
and that all this is just talk
oh we know

that it's just not good enough to live things down
and that we are going to live them down all the same
oh we know oh we know

that there is nothing new in all this
and that life is wonderful
and that's all there is to it
oh we know all this perfectly well

and that we know all this perfectly well
oh we know that too
oh we know it
oh we know

Assembly Line

Shu Ting
translated from the Chinese by Carolyn Kizer

In time's assembly line
Night presses against night.
We come off the factory night-shift
In line as we march towards home.
Over our heads in a row
The assembly line of stars
Stretches across the sky.
Beside us, little trees
Stand numb in assembly lines.

The stars must be exhausted
After thousands of years
Of journeys which never change.
The little trees are all sick,
Choked on smog and monotony,
Stripped of their color and shape.
It's not hard to feel for them;
We share the same tempo and rhythm.

Yes, I'm numb to my own existence
As if, like the trees and stars
—perhaps just out of habit
—perhaps just out of sorrow,
I'm unable to show concern
For my own manufactured fate.

Gifts

Shu Ting
translated from the Chinese by Carolyn Kizer

My dream is the dream of a pond
Not just to mirror the sky
But to let the willows and ferns
Suck me dry.
I'll climb from the roots to the veins,
And when leaves wither and fade
I will refuse to mourn
Because I was dying to live.

My joy is the joy of sunlight.
In a moment of creation
I will leave shining words
In the pupils of children's eyes
Igniting golden flames.
Whenever seedlings sprout
I shall sing a song of green.
I'm so simple I'm profound!

My grief is the grief of birds.
The Spring will understand:
Flying from hardship and failure
To a future of warmth and light.
There my blood-stained pinions
Will scratch hieroglyphics
On every human heart
For every year to come.

Because all that I am
Has been a gift from earth.

Fairy Tales

Shu Ting
translated from the Chinese by Donald Finkel

You believed in your own story,
then climbed inside it—
a turquoise flower.
You gazed past ailing trees,
past crumbling walls and rusty railings.
Your least gesture beckoned a constellation
of wild vetch, grasshoppers, and stars
to sweep you into immaculate distances.

The heart may be tiny
but the world's enormous.

And the people in turn believe—
in pine trees after rain,
ten thousand tiny suns, a mulberry branch
bent over water like a fishing-rod,
a cloud tangled in the tail of a kite.
Shaking off dust, in silver voices
ten thousand memories sing from your dream.

The world may be tiny
but the heart's enormous.

Hold Fast Your Dreams

Louise Driscoll

Hold fast your dreams!
Within your heart
Keep one still, secret spot
Where dreams may go,
And, sheltered so,
May thrive and grow—
Where doubt and fear are not.
O keep a place apart,
Within your heart,
For little dreams to go!

Think still of lovely things that are not true.
Let wish and magic work at will in you.
Be sometimes blind to sorrow. Make believe!
Forget the calm that lies
In disillusioned eyes.
Though we all know that we must die,
Yet you and I
May walk like gods and be
Even now at home in immortality.

We see so many ugly things
Deceits and wrongs and quarrelings;
We know, alas! We know
How quickly fade
The color in the west,
The bloom upon thc brcast
And youth's blind hour.
Yet keep within your heart
A place apart
Where little dreams may go,
May thrive and grow.
Hold fast—hold fast your dreams!

From *Best Loved Poems to Read Again and Again.*

Harlem

Langston Hughes

What happens to a dream deferred?

Does it dry up
like a raisin in the sun?
Or fester like a sore?
And then run?
Does it stink like rotten meat?
Or crust and sugar over?
like syrupy sweet?

Maybe it just sags
like a heavy load.

Or does it explode?

My Heart Leaps Up

William Wordsworth

My heart leaps up when I behold
    A rainbow in the sky:
So was it when my life began;
So is it now I am a man;
So be it when I shall grow old,
    Or let me die!
The Child is father of the Man;
And I could wish my days to be
Bound each to each by natural piety.

Daffodils

William Wordsworth

I wandered lonely as a cloud
    That floats on high o'er vales and hills,
When all at once I saw a crowd,
    A host, of golden daffodils;
Beside the lake, beneath the trees,
Fluttering and dancing in the breeze.

Continuous as the stars that shone
    And twinkle on the Milky Way,
They stretched in never-ending line
    Along the margin of a bay:
Ten thousand saw I at a glance,
Tossing their heads in sprightly dance.

The waves beside them danced, but they
    Out-did the sparkling waves in glee:
A poet could not but be gay,
    In such a jocund company:
I gazed—and gazed—but little thought
What wealth the show to me had brought:

For oft, when on my couch I lie
    In vacant or in pensive mood,
They flash upon that inward eye
    Which is the bliss of solitude;
And then my heart with pleasure fills,
And dances with the daffodils.

Spring

Thomas Nashe

Spring, the sweet spring, is the year's pleasant king;
Then blooms each thing, then maids dance in a ring,
Cold doth not sting, the pretty birds do sing:
    Cuckoo, jug-jug, pu-we, to-witta-woo!

The palm and may make country houses gay,
Lambs frisk and play, the shepherds pipe all day,
And we hear aye birds tune this merry lay:
    Cuckoo, jug-jug, pu-we, to-witta-woo!

The fields breathe sweet, the daisies kiss our feet,
Young lovers meet, old wives a-sunning sit;
In every street these tunes our ears do greet:
    Cuckoo, jug-jug, pu-we, to-witta-woo!
        Spring, the sweet spring!

From *Summer's Last Will and Testament*, 1600.

People Liked Him

Edgar Guest

People liked him, not because
He was rich or known to fame;
He had never won applause
As a star in any game.
His was not a brilliant style,
His was not a forceful way,
But he had a gentle smile
And a kindly word to say.

Never arrogant or proud,
On he went with manner mild;
Never quarrelsome or loud,
Just as simple as a child;
Honest, patient, brave and true:
Thus he lived from day to day,
Doing what he found to do
In a cheerful sort of way.

Wasn't one to boast of gold
Or belittle it with sneers,
Didn't change from hot to cold,
Kept his friends throughout the years,
Sort of man you like to meet
Any time or any place.
There was always something sweet
And refreshing in his face.

Sort of man you'd like to be:
Balanced well and truly square;
Patient in adversity,
Generous when his skies were fair.
Never lied to friend or foe,
Never rash in word or deed,
Quick to come and slow to go
In a neighbor's time of need.

From *Best Loved Poems to Read Again and Again.*

Never rose to wealth or fame,
    Simply lived, and simply died,
But passing of his name
    Left a sorrow, far and wide.
Not for glory he'd attained,
    Nor for what he had of pelf,
Were the friends that he had gained,
    But for what he was himself.

If

Rudyard Kipling

If you can keep your head when all about you
Are losing theirs and blaming it on you;
If you can trust yourself when all men doubt you,
But make allowance for their doubting too;
If you can wait and not be tired by waiting,
Or, being lied about, don't deal in lies,
Or, being hated, don't give way to hating,
And yet don't look too good, nor talk too wise;

If you can dream—and not make dreams your master;
If you can think—and not make thought your aim;
If you can meet with triumph and disaster
And treat those two impostors just the same;
If you can bear to hear the truth you've spoken
Twisted by knaves to make a trap for fools,
Or watch the things you gave your life to broken,
And stoop and build 'em up with worn out tools;

If you can make one heap of all your winnings
And risk it on one turn of pitch-and -toss,
And lose, and start again at the beginnings
And never breathe a word about your loss;
If you can fore your heart and nerve and sinew
To serve your turn long after they are gone,
And so hold on when there is nothing in you
Except the Will which says to them: "Hold on!"

If you can talk with crowds and keep your virtue,
Or walk with kings—nor lose the common touch;
If neither foes nor loving friends can hurt you;
If all men count with you, but none too much;
If you can fill the unforgiving minute
With sixty seconds worth of distance run
Yours is the Earth and everything that's in it,
And—which is more—you'll be a Man, my son!

From *Rudyard Kipling's Verse,* Inclusive Edition, 1920, Doubleday.

A Perfect Day

Carrie Jacobs Bond

When you come to the end of a perfect day
    And you sit alone with your thought
While the chimes ring out with a carol gay
    For the joy that the day has brought,
Do you think what the end of a perfect day
    Can mean to a tired heart?
When the sun goes down with a flaming ray
    And the dear friends have to part?

Well, this is the end of a perfect day,
    Near the end of a journey, too;
But it leaves a thought that is big and strong,
    With a wish that is kind and true;
For mem'ry has painted this perfect day
    With colors that never fade,
And we find, at the end of a perfect day,
    The soul of a friend we've made.

From *Songs Everybody Sings* by Carrie Jacobs-Bond, Boston Music Company, 1925.

Do Not Go Gentle into That Good Night

Dylan Thomas

Do not go gentle into that good night,
Old age should burn and rave at close of day;
Rage, rage against the dying of the light.

Though wise men at their end know dark is right,
Because their words had forked no lightning they
Do not go gentle into that good night.

Good men, the last wave by, crying how bright
Their frail deeds might have danced in a green bay,
Rage, rage against the dying of the light.

Wild men who caught and sang the sun in flight,
And learn, too late, they grieved it on its way,
Do not go gentle into that good night.

Grave men, near death, who see with blinding sight
Blind eyes could blaze like meteors and be gay,
Rage, rage against the dying of the light.

And you, the father, there on the sad height,
Curse, bless, me now with your fierce tears, I pray.
Do not go gentle into that good night.
Rage, rage against the dying of the light.